CHILE REDISCOVERED

The author wishes to thank two of his Chilean friends:
Dominique Hachette and Chantal Montero Pradte.
Also, London Library for procuring rare books
on the Aymara language, and Mildred Marney
of Rowan Script for deciphering his handwriting
and correcting slips and blunders.

CHILE REDISCOVERED

In Search of Eden

Vincent Cronin

STACEY
INTERNATIONAL

Published by
Stacey International
128 Kensington Church Street
London W8 4BH
Tel: +44 (0)20 7221 7166 Fax: +44 (0)20 7792 9288
E-mail: info@stacey-international.co.uk
www.stacey-international.co.uk

© Vincent Cronin 2009

ISBN: 9781906768027

Printed and bound in Great Britain

British Library Catalogue in Publication Data:
A catalogue record for this book is available from
the British Library.

Contents

Chile Rediscovered is framed by a journey seen as taking place some time after the end of the Pinochet regime yet when the long shadow of its authority still falls across the land.

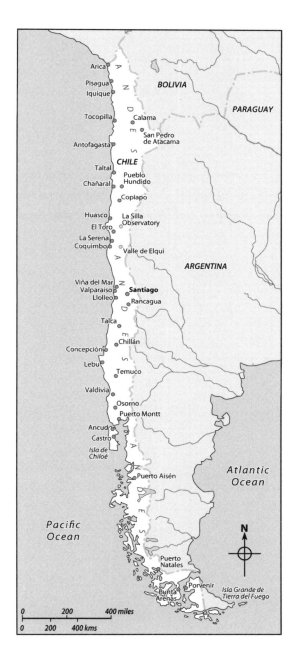

Arica
Pisagua
Iquique
Tocopilla
Calama
San Pedro
de Atacama
Antofagasta
CHILE
Taltal
Pueblo
Hundido
Chañaral
Copiapo
Huasco
La Silla
Observatory
El Toro
La Serena
Coquimbo
Valle de Elqui
ARGENTINA
Viña del Mar
Valparaiso
Santiago
Llolleo
Rancagua
Talca
Chillán
Concepción
Lebu
Temuco
Valdivia
Osorno
Puerto Montt
Ancud
Castro
Isla de
Chiloé
Puerto Aisén
BOLIVIA
PARAGUAY
Atlantic
Ocean
Pacific
Ocean
N
Puerto
Natales
Porvenir
Punta
Arenas
Isla Grande de
Tierra del Fuego

0   200   400 miles
0   200   400 kms

NORTHERN
CHILE

SOUTHERN
CHILE

viii

An Unexpected Summons

I still remember that September morning several years ago when a forgotten name came back into my life. I got up at six and set to work in a dressing gown making last-minute changes to the plans of a country house I had been commissioned to design. The buyer had once again changed his mind: this time the garage must be enlarged – to hold three, instead of two, cars. This was going to spoil the studied rhythm of the north façade. Against the grain, I pencilled in, then inked, the modifications.

A cold front had arrived and the house was unheated till eight. I warmed a mug of coffee and turned to work I enjoyed. As consultant to our town and country planning commisssion, I was in charge of a big housing scheme connected to the projected bypass for our market town. I intended the house fronts to be aligned in harmony with the landscape contours opposite. That way, brick and glass would reflect back to nature some of the beauty their occupants enjoyed. But I could already hear the voices of protest. 'How much extra will this cost?'

I heard the postman's feet on the drive and went to pick up the handful of circulars and bills plus one airmail envelope. The stamp was foreign and the rather blurred postmark read Santiago. Whom did I know in Spain? No one.

It was addressed to my parents' former home, sold recently to pay death duties, and had been forwarded by the new owner. Odd. I slit open the thin envelope with a butter knife, unfolded the single sheet and stared at the signature, large, bold and legible in dark blue gel: Gonzalo.

Gonzalo! I spoke it out loud, the two last syllables fading like an echo. An echo from the past. When had I first seen him? Ten, eleven years before, arriving in England with a letter of recommendation to my father from his business counterpart in Paris. Aged twenty-three, strongly built, an almost penniless political exile from Pinochet's Chile.

He stayed in our house for a week, never alluding to his months in prison, always speaking well of Chile and his fellow Chileans. His ambition was to study for a degree in geology, with a view to tapping Chile's rich mineral resources if he could ever return. It so happened that my own degree at Imperial College in construction engineering included a course in seismology where faculty members were involved with Andean tectonics. After enlisting their help, I was able to get Gonzalo a place, perhaps influenced by sympathy for his stand against Pinochet.

We invited him to stay in the summer vacation. Intrigued by our fondness for croquet, he spent hours on the lawn learning and practising until, by his last day, he'd become unbeatable. Patriotism and perseverance: these won him respect.

The letter was typed under an embossed heading: Commissariat for National Resources, Office of the Executive Director.

Dear Archie,

Pollution in our capital has increased to the point where we must plan for a massive residential overflow development south of the River Mapocho.

I've set up a first-rate advisory committee to begin assessing possible sites, but we still lack expert opinion. Our Ambassador in London recommended you.

We have a meeting planned for the last fortnight in September. Would you be free and willing to come here, air fares and expenses paid? No croquet, but a warm welcome.

Please telephone me on my private line at the number above.

Affectionately,
Gonzalo

I hadn't given a thought to Gonzalo since his return to Chile and I was pleased he now held an interesting job and was making me this friendly offer. The proposal needed mulling over, and this meant fresh air and one of my 'pro or con' walks.

I knew most of Britain well, but the furthest I'd travelled in Europe was Florence, where I went to shovel mud when the Arno burst its banks. About Chile I had no special feeling apart from relief that Pinochet had gone at last. I felt I could do with a break and I had fewer commitments at home, my wife being much absorbed by an advanced computer course nearby and our daughter at Art School in Glasgow.

Making allowance for the eight-hour time difference, I called Gonzalo at eight that evening. It was good to hear his warm baritone, its delivery now much more assured. He answered all my queries about climate, clothes, journey. Then came an added surprise. He urged me to come well before the committee meeting so he could take me on a whistle-stop tour of his country. Nothing to pay: I would be his guest, at Government expense. I had to think fast. The offer was tempting and the trip would doubtless be educative. I agreed. He sounded pleased and said he would send me the tickets the next day.

A month later I found myself in Puerto Montt, a sleepy fishing port an hour and a half's flight south of Santiago. The town had been much battered by a recent earthquake: what had fallen and what had survived, sometimes astonishingly intact, absorbed my attention. It was late spring, the sun shone, flowers and fruit were arrayed in the market stalls. A cold wind blew in from the Pacific and reminded me that I was hungry.

I chose a small restaurant facing the sea, patronized by sailors and fishermen. Sitting down at the one vacant table set for two, I ordered sea bass and a bottle of Chilean beer.

A tall slim man came in carrying a large leather suitcase with brass locks. After taking in the crowded room, he approached my table.

'Pardon, Monsieur, est-ce que c'est libre?'

I spread a hand invitingly, at which he inclined his head. High brow, thinning black hair combed back smoothly, a small unostentatious moustache, authoritative air.

Taking the seat opposite, he removed kid gloves and studied the menu. I noted his smart collar, sober tie and pin holding the knot in place. When his order of sea bass arrived, he deftly eased off the skin with his knife, removing the backbone with a flick of his wrist before extracting the ticklish bones near the head. Only then did he begin eating.

I waited till he'd finished and ordered coffee. 'Do you happen to know Gonzalo?'

He looked at me cautiously. 'Why do you ask?'

'Gonzalo mentioned a Frenchman would be joining us on board the *Puerto Eden*.'

His face relaxed and he introduced himself. 'Docteur de Coudray… And you perhaps will be… Archie?'

'Yes and no! The man who betrayed Gonzalo and landed him in prison was a Vincenzo, so Gonzalo hates calling me Vincent and uses my middle name instead.'

He considered this. 'Since we're travelling together, may I do the same? Friends call me Bernard.'

'Agreed. And I'm so relieved you speak English. The few Frenchmen I've met take the line of Victor Hugo. When living in Jersey as a political exile, he refused to give interviews in English. "But English is the language of your beloved Shakespeare," people protested. At which he would draw himself up. "Those who talk to Victor Hugo must speak the language of Victor Hugo."'

He smiled, whereupon his moustache lengthened in a way I found Chaplinesque. 'Times change. I learned English because my research papers have to be submitted in unpoetic English, the *lingua franca* of scientists.'

Over coffee he told me how he'd come to know Gonzalo. It was in Paris, when Bernard was a doctor in the Necker hospital and had found Gonzalo working as a poorly paid porter wheeling patients on trolleys from ward to operating theatre, scanner or morgue. Learning that he was a political refugee and well educated, Bernard was curious to know him, liked his optimism and was particularly impressed that Gonzalo wouldn't hear a word spoken against his country or people. Bernard found him a better paid job in the hospital, but French immigration law determined he could stay no longer, whereupon Gonzalo chose to try his luck in England.

It was time to collect my luggage, left with an obliging hotel porter. Passing the mooring pool for small motorized fishing boats, ten minutes' walk brought us level with sheds and depositories serving the still invisible deep sea harbour. We eventually found the boarding stage of the *Puerto Eden* where we looked out at the ocean but there was no sign of our ship.

At the counter a friendly youth listened uneasily to our enquiry. 'Your ship has sailed… half an hour ago,' he blurted.

'But she was due to leave at eight.'

This brought a decisive shake of the head.

'When is the next sailing?' asked Bernard carefully.

'A week from now.'

Much annoyed, we produced our tickets.

'The agency made a mistake.' Apparently not for the first time.

At that moment Gonzalo hurried in slightly out of breath. He placed a hand on Bernard's shoulder before embracing me in a quick bear hug. He had broadened while his face had slimmed, with new anxiety lines on brow and jaw. Still the same were his lively hazel eyes, with their assured, outgoing expression.

He examined our tickets and quickly took charge. Calling for a telephone, he spoke to the harbour master, firm but friendly. Our ship had not yet cleared harbour; there might just be time to board her.

Five minutes later, we jumped into the tug, caught our luggage as it was lobbed across, then ducked geyser-like spray as the tug opened full throttle and bucked seaward.

The *Puerto Eden* proved to be a three-deck ship of 5,000 tonnes with a stern that lifted for drive-on trucks. She had lowered a wooden boarding ladder with a crewman ready to pull us on; we scrambled up, cheered by watching passengers.

I expressed my relief to Bernard who surprised me by saying, 'Boarding a ship after she's sailed, that's a bad omen. Very bad.'

Having deposited our baggage in the four-bunk cabin reserved for us, Gonzalo invited us to view our ship, a cargo he emphasized, passengers were merely subsidiary. A heavy-duty iron lift took us down to the main hold where a dozen large trucks stood tight parked. They had been driven onboard along a retractable iron gangway. Stacked under roped-down tarpaulins lay sacks of cement, machinery, batteries, flour, sugar and suchlike necessities. Drivers shared a big cabin and messed with the crew. Gonzalo explained that there was one north-south road which ran down alongside the Andes, but it was only suitable for cars and was interrupted by a river with no regular ferry. So, in the absence of any land route between Chile's hips and her Patagonian feet, this ship had been making the link for the previous twenty years.

We climbed upstairs, ventilators sucking wind into the engine room, twin funnels clearing it of fumes, life rafts and lifeboats suspended from derricks. When Bernard pointed to rust on the derricks and companion ladders, Gonzalo reacted sharply. This was a working ship, not a millionaire's yacht. She was sound and insured with Lloyd's.

On the bridge, the captain greeted Gonzalo and indicated our intended route on a spread-out chart. Then he pointed out our present position between mainland and the large island of Chiloé on a map showing in relief the mountainous indentations of the coastline. We had entered a succession of channels which Chile had turned into one of the world's largest, shallowest and most dangerous waterways. The maps came as a surprise to Bernard and me: from our home atlases, we had pictured Chile as a long lean stretch of land between the Andes cordillera and the Pacific Ocean. Not so. Starting with Chiloé, we could see how the coast had crumbled into hundreds of rocks and islets for a distance of 1,500 kilometres before finishing at Cape Horn, the point of Chile's foot. Our ship would be navigating between these islets for the next two days and nights.

I had left Santiago under a blue sky and hot sun; here, 900 kilometres south, grey cirrus and a light cold breeze halved the temperature to 16 degrees. Our ship was skirting Chiloé, close enough to spot a village and give us a feel for the terrain. Gonzalo put us in the picture, describing the Mapuche, the country's largest indigenous tribe. He said their women were strong and aggressive, with some looking like champion wrestlers. In past times, they rode their horses bareback and attacked the Spaniards with pointed lances. In complete contrast to other South American tribes, Mapuche women played a major role: only they communicated with the gods of life and death. Unlike the Incas and Aztecs, they had no central government: power lay instead with the *cacique* of each family, and each family might number up to five hundred members. The Mapuche grazed animals, hunted and fished and lived in huts which they moved with the seasons.

Bernard had his binoculars trained on the island's coastline. 'Why do they build their huts on stilts?'

'As rising tidewaters roar in through the tiny channel of Chacao, which we've just passed,' said Gonzalo, sweeping his hands through the air, 'they clash with tides coming in from a southern channel. This creates huge whirlpools and waves, very dangerous for small boats. The difference between high and low tides is seven metres. If those wooden houses weren't raised on stilts, they would flood or even smash.'

Bernard lowered his binoculars and turned to Gonzalo. 'I read somewhere that Chile was fortunate to have so many missionaries come here from all over Europe ever since the first Spaniards arrived.'

'Chiloé was their biggest success. Jesuits arrived early in the seventeenth century. No roads, so they travelled along the coast in small boats manned by two missionaries. They would start their annual rounds from Castro with three portable altars, Mass vestments, banners of Christ and the rest. After they'd evangelized one part of the coast, they would build a chapel. During their two hundred-year stay here, they built no less than one hundred chapels, which gives you an idea of the numbers of conversions. That should gratify you, Archie! All those souls saved by the Church of Rome! Some of the buildings have soaring belfries – the German Jesuits chose Bavarian architecture as their model and used local wooden shingle for roof and walls. The churches have survived two centuries of rain and salt mist and are still used for seasonal religious ceremonies.

'This may interest you, Archie,' he rattled on. 'Chiloé became a royalist stronghold during the wars of independence in the early nineteenth century. The Spanish Governor of Chile fled to Chiloé and despairingly offered the island to England's King George. The offer was declined and Chiloé surrendered to the Republic of Chile in 1826.'

I laughed. 'Wise old George IV! Might have landed us in another Falklands War.'

We were beginning to feel hungry and at seven sharp made for the cafeteria. Gonzalo chatted up those already queuing. They ranged from a two year-old boy to a white-haired septuagenarian and his young wife, mostly Europeans but with a sprinkling of North Americans; they were bent on seeing the sights of South Chile. No one seemed quite sure which sight or sights but they all seemed agreed that three days on the *Puerto Eden* was an experience not to be missed.

Gonzalo told us about the island's exceptionally rich folklore. He said Chilotans believe in a secret brotherhood of male witches organized into an underground of councils which meet in cleverly disguised caves. They come dressed as birds and wearing the luminous *macuñ*, made from the skin off a virgin's chest, which enables them to fly. Witches also steer the *Caleuche*, a ghost ship which takes on a cargo of doomed guests caught up in an eternal party. To the haunting strain of accordion music, the crew recover the bodies of those who have died at sea. The ship travels veiled in cloud and always at night and can descend beneath the waves, disappearing when someone comes too close. 'If caught looking at the *Caleuche*, beware!' he warned; 'your mouth will become twisted, your head crooked or else you'll suddenly die.'

Bernard shrugged and puckered his lips. 'Every seagoing culture has its mystery ship. This tells us nothing about the Chilotans who are presumably mostly Christian.'

Gonzalo nodded. 'No doubt these stories belong to an earlier culture when the islanders were simple fisher-folk, terrified by racing tides and horrendous earthquakes for which Chiloé is infamous.'

Next morning the sea was flat. Bernard and I went forward to join youngsters looking out for land. We spotted occasional sea-birds but it was mammals Bernard had journeyed across the globe to see.

'Sea otter!' shouted a sharp-eyed boy.

He pointed. A small blackish head had broken the surface and was bobbing gently.

Bernard swung his binoculars and caught it momentarily. The head went under. He looked at his watch. 'Eleven thirty-two. Perhaps a sea-otter, perhaps not. We'll soon see.'

The surface remained blank. Some of those watching drifted away. Twice we thought we saw faint ripples: fish feeding. 'There he is!' cried out Bernard, quickly focusing on a dark blob. 'Not a sea otter. A seal.'

'How can you tell?' I asked.

'By my watch. A sea otter is limited by the breath in its lungs to half a minute underwater. Seals can remain much longer. This chap dived for five minutes plus.'

'All on a single deep breath?'

Bernard turned towards me and straightened his back. 'Red pigment absorbs the oxygen we breathe and circulates it to our body. The seal possesses much larger quantities of red pigment than land animals and therefore has more oxygen in his blood stream. Before he dives, he shuts off his lungs and slows his flow of blood. The oxygen stored in his red pigment keeps him active for up to five minutes or so.'

'You've studied seals?'

'No. But my special field is leukaemia, so I have to be *au fait* with all types of blood. Of human blood alone, there are twenty-seven different types.'

Passing through the seating area, I found Gonzalo giving a talk to any interested passengers. He spoke of the years of hard work that had gone into charting and designing the world's longest natural waterway; of how Chile was the only true democracy in all South America; of how she would build on her reputation for peacemaking and make her future from her mineral resources. What a change from the student of earlier years! When I had first known him, he had been tense, unsure of himself, fearful of remaining an exile, but still avid to learn from England's political system anything that could be useful in Chile. He had filled out physically, the lean cheeks rounded, auburn hair brushed back; he held himself straight, head high.

In the late afternoon we left the shelter of Chiloé and faced the full force of the Pacific. The ship began to buck high waves. Bernard immediately went to our cabin and, without undressing, stretched out on his bunk, eyes closed. Gonzalo tried to persuade him to come up on deck and walk with his head into the wind. 'Useless,' replied Bernard without moving. 'Seasickness is caused by imbalance in the inner ear.'

So we left him, Gonzalo to go to the seating area, I to walk up and down the deck for half an hour. Then the wind became too strong for me and I spent part of the night pacing the dimly lit corridor outside our cabin like a trapped rodent.

Next morning the wind had dropped and the sea was nearly calm. Leaving the Pacific, we entered waters partly protected by islets to both starboard and port, many of them densely wooded with a variety of trees including monkey-puzzle araucarias. I stood on deck wondering aloud about the land-forms about us. Were these islets the tips of mountains submerged by an almighty flood? Or were they newer peaks erupted from now extinct volcanoes? Bernard declined to give an opinion.

My imagination remained gripped by the mysterious landscape. Mist hid the sun's disc, cooled its rays and muffled the mountainous coast. Ahead stretched a spacious avenue of smooth water with here and there small islands dense with evergreen trees. We'd been told that man had never set foot here. Our engines, at 'Dead Slow', were hushed, a mere heartbeat. Our sharp prow cut the smoothness, lifting a wisp of white and a stir of air to our foredeck, cautiously venturing into whatever lay ahead. To port, by moments mist thinned to reveal what might be mountain slopes or perhaps banks of cumulus, only to thicken before I could tell.

A scene as strange to me as a foreign tongue, yet haunting as a Caspar David Friedrich painting: a man in the foreground gazes at an awesome landscape, but we see only the back of his head, for his self has momentarily been lost in what he sees.

I had hoped Chile would offer new experiences and here was one already. Why were we travelling 'Dead Slow' when the sea was calm and no other ship entered the channel? And these islands where no man ventured, did they belong to an Earth still being shaped, greyish clay from the hands of the potter? Where were we said to be heading in our ship with its motley of strangers, one to another, in the hands of a silent crew? If we were going South – towards Tierra del Fuego, the end of the Earth – why on the bridge hadn't they named our destination port? Was there no destination? Or, if there was, were we destined not to reach it? Lines by Hopkins came to mind: a German passenger ship wrecked in a storm: loss of 120 souls. Not lives, souls. Could it be that our almost silent ship was carrying souls on their most important voyage of all – across a wider Styx – outward bound?

A firm hand gripped my shoulder. I started and turned. Gonzalo was smiling. 'You seemed quite engrossed. What do you make of it?'

For me, friendship is also about sharing new experience, and I shared this one.

Gonzalo looked surprised, then reproving. 'Why say it's new? You're reviving long ago experiences of art and poetry to ease the shock of novelty.'

'What's so wrong about that?'

'Because you're here as a traveller, a would-be discoverer of *differences* as between one country and its people and another.' He closed his eyes and rubbed his wrist against his forehead. 'A lapse on my part. Should have explained myself better. We know well enough that Chile's coast is a battleground for two massive tectonic plates moving in opposite directions. Hence earth tremors and violent eruptions in the ocean bed. One such caused a massive rise in the ocean level and drowned a large chunk of coast. These rocks tufted with firs are not islands: they are tips of mountains on the far side of which was a valley, now the channel. That's why it's so shallow.'

CHAPTER TWO

Eden

Early next morning we sighted the mainland; our engines slowed and eventually stopped. Two of our crew hurried forward to release the anchor which then dropped lazily with massive clanking of chain. A ladder was lowered to port, cartons and provisions loaded onto a stout rowboat and duly carried to the local store which served woodsmen felling trees further inland.

Gonzalo explained why the place was called Puerto Eden. 'Sixty years ago prospectors looking for a suitable landing place discovered a few families living here. Small of stature, speaking a language peculiar to themselves, they collected limpets and other molluscs from the rocks, hunted seal with wooden spears and caught fish with fibre lines. And they went about completely naked.' He opened his wallet and showed us a photograph taken by his great-uncle. Three stocky adult men, one woman, two children, all seated on a bench as Mother Nature had made them. They wore the solemn expressions of a passport pose.

'In winter,' Gonzalo continued, 'the water temperature drops to near zero. They swam and dived for shellfish and protected themselves by smearing their bodies with seal oil.'

'Could that really keep out the cold?' I asked.

'Applied often enough, it can alter the consistency of the epidermis, toughening and insulating the skin. Seal fat in their diet would help too, like with Eskimos.'

Gonzalo continued, 'Nudity is common enough in hot countries, but these fishermen were perhaps unique in braving cold. Unique too in being naked hunters and gatherers. Each family lived on its own small boat, moving from one fishing ground to another.' He said they were peaceable people living in primal innocence, deeply attached to their children, whom they called *peteet*. Hence the name Eden, or Puerto Eden as it became.

These nomadic fishermen struck a chord with me. When I was preparing for my journey to Chile, I had studied the British Navy's charting of the South Pacific and come across a little-read report in a learned journal. I shared this now with my friends. I recounted how the ingenuity of the natives had been noted by a young English naval officer, John Byron, later to become grandfather to the poet. His ship, the *Wager*, was wrecked far down the coast. The crew mutinied and took their chance southward. Byron and the captain trekked north and met with the sea nomads. They proved friendly to the exhausted strangers and took Byron onto one of their boats. It consisted of five planks, one for the bottom and two for each side. Having no iron tools, they would hack a trunk or a single board out of a large tree using shells and flints, and with the help of fire. Along the edges of the boards they made small holes and bound them together with woodbine and bark mashed to make a substitute oakum. To avoid doubling back to capes and headlands fatal to any open boat, they would dismantle the parts with each man or woman carrying a piece of the boat.

On his boat, Byron was set to an oar. He removed his hat and placed it beside him and, every now and then, he ate a limpet, as others were doing. One of them, seeing Byron throw the shells overboard, spoke to the rest in a violent passion, then fell upon him and, seizing him by a ragged handkerchief he had about his neck, almost throttled him. Another took hold of his legs and was going to throw him overboard if an old woman had not intervened. Byron had no idea why he had given offence till he noticed that others in the boat carefully heaped the empty limpet shells in the hull. I rounded off the account with a question. 'Byron couldn't explain their sudden violence. Can we?'

'Ritual cleanliness?' Bernard suggested. 'Yet they were keeping unwashed shells, sticky with filaments and a bait for flies. Some fish shells are useful as razors but not I think limpets.'

Gonzalo intervened. 'Byron couldn't know it but these Alcalufe have many stories. One of them is about a powerful water fairy who long ago warned her people never to throw their used shells back in the water. Should they do so, fish would shun the spot forever. Instead, they were to pile shells on the nearest shore and, when the pile grew high, they were to move to new waters. These nomads manage not to deplete fish stocks by self-regulation. Our governments resort to money payments for the same end.'

I asked Gonzalo why the Alcalufe had left Eden for nearby inlets.

'Like Adam and Eve, they were driven out.' He paused, suddenly glum. He explained how a few white Chileans had settled there to construct the landing stage. From the best of motives, they provided the nomads with woollen vests and cotton trousers and persuaded them to wear these. Diving often and living in open boats with no shelter from the rain, their vests were permanently sodden and they soon contracted pneumonia. Several died. Suspecting their would-be benefactors of black magic, the Alcalufe stripped off their clothes and rowed to less dangerous waters.

'So they disappeared?' I asked.

'Yes and no. They haven't been seen since for the good reason that these fjord-like waters are unnavigable by our type of boat, and the thickly wooded rocky cays are impassable. From time to time we find a newly heaped pile of shells. We know the sea nomads are still alive and fishing.'

Mestizos were drifting out of the shore huts. Two pairs carrying oars boarded the row boats and made for our lower deck, there to barter with interested crewmen: much esteemed abalone-type molluscs for tobacco and matches. Meanwhile our engines were being given the once-over and the ropes lashing cargo to the lower deck, which had been loosened in rough weather, were being tightened.

A sudden loud clanking of heavy chains as winches aft turned to weigh anchor. Slowly we glided away from this tiny dot on a map but the sepia image of those vulnerable fishermen stayed with me.

Early next morning I stood on the foredeck and admired what I saw. To port rose the mountainous mainland, now with snow-capped peaks, to starboard a scattering of islands, some with a beach heaped with shells, most thick with evergreen trees, all unpenetrated. It was late spring but low grey cloud brought a wintry look to the calm sea. Ahead the dark waters of the narrow channel. All was silent save for the slish of our prow cleaving the calm at six knots. The setting was unlike any other I had known: it was austere and gaunt yet perhaps because the air was mild it did not strike me as hostile. No colours but shades of grey and black.

Bernard had told me he would be going to the bridge and I decided to see what he was up to. I found him with the officer in charge of the echo-sounding machine. This signalled the depth of water beneath the ship with numbers on a screen. It had been devised in the Second World War to detect and sink enemy submarines. Bernard was explaining in schoolboy Spanish how the same principle was now used to save lives in his hospital. 'Bone no longer conceals the marrow inside. We've actually become transparent!' Then he turned smiling to me. 'Now we can't help but praise "transparency" and take pride in revealing the failings which we used to reserve for the confessional!'

The wide avenue of misty sea dotted with tufted rocks had been slowly narrowing and now on both sides land drew close, treeless and with scant vegetation of any sort. Our clearance dropped to under a fathom as we swung into the first of two bends. The captain told us to leave the bridge.

We found places on the leeward side of the same deck where we had a clear view ahead and could still hear the officer calling out numbers, as if in a lottery, for the wheel to be moved a fraction.

We were now in a channel not much wider than a barge canal: inviting waterways opened on either side, one leading to the Pacific to battle with the Humbolt Current, the other inland, where rising ground would close it off. Constantly trifurcating and, with bends becoming sharper and more frequent, the channel resembled a maze.

We came to a bend where black buoys bobbed at intervals on the port side warning us off invisible rocks. The ship was inching forward. A bearded passenger beside me remarked darkly, 'Enter by the narrow gate. But what if you're blind and your guide dog's asleep?'

The channel curved again and, to our surprise, opened upon high ground immediately ahead and very close. What looked like a large island lay mid-stream, blocking our passage. We headed straight for the island and looked like ramming it but, at the last moment, veered sharply to port. Hugging its rocky edge, where there would be deeper clearance, we kept on this course to find it wasn't an island at all but a high cape jutting from land to the west. We rounded it and saw the narrows that lay clear ahead.

I breathed relief and fantasized a sequel. Had we run aground and our ship foundered, perhaps the hidden but ever watchful Alcalufe would have made themselves known and ferried us back to Eden.

Dusk faded to night and still we held our course. Evidently we couldn't afford to drop anchor and lose twelve hours, for which the crew would have to be paid. Even in this remote landscape man was subject to cost constraints.

On our last morning aboard, we woke to find we had left the narrows and were heading east into the sound named Ultima Esperanza, last safe anchorage before Cape Horn. Soon we sighted the wharves and wooden houses with corrugated iron roofs of Puerto Natales, yet mooring proved as measured as departure had been fraught. A sharp wind from the Pacific had blown up, forcing our ship to circle the outer harbour twice before daring to sidle up to the single landing stage to be secured with hawsers. Soon the broad gangway was lowered to let off the trucks on the lower decks loaded with their commodities. Only then did we descend in the iron hoist and set foot in Chile's southernmost region.

Here at last would we meet the grandeur of the southern Andes.

CHAPTER THREE

A Destructive Wind

Bernard welcomed the sight of terra firma by starting to sing to himself. His relief proved rather premature: instead of heading for town, where our baggage awaited collection, Gonzalo steered us towards an inland waterway. Soon we met up with an inflatable dinghy: the sailor-owner helped bundle us onboard. On his third attempt, the boatman fired the outboard engine and we chugged slowly into a broad expanse of calm water. Groups of seals and sea lions sprawled on rocky outcrops; here and there porpoises broke the surface and performed for us.

Ahead, stark against a blue sky, soared three granite peaks honed by wind and weather into rudimentary towers. These were the Torres del Paine, 2,800 metres high, the southernmost fling of the immense Andes range which, like a mammoth's vertebrae, supports the whole attenuated body of Chile.

The towers stand guard over three snow-clad precipices and lower shale hills which dangle silver threads of waterfall. Below lie lakes, their colours ranging from grey to bright blue and Nile green, depending on the nature of the inflowing silt.

We were now well into the waterway. Its banks steepened to a cliff at the far end, down which hung a spill of gleaming ice. Rather than heading for the cliff, Gonzalo signalled to cut the motor and our boatman paddled us to a suitable landing point. Once ashore, we had to climb up awkward scree, slithering on loose stones and grabbing support from low bushes. Ten minutes' scramble brought us up to where we could see what lay beyond.

There it burst on us: a grey-white basin wide as the Thames at Wapping, sweeping down from a distant mountainside. Immense, probably many kilometres long, dominant yet also lacking any kind of shape. Compared to the distant peaks clear-cut against the sky, this was sprawl, earthbound, lustreless, hiding its identity, almost reptilian. Or could it be something that by rights should not exist, a chunk of anti-nature? The place exuded a tomb-like chill.

Gonzalo surveyed the scene and, lifting one arm, offered us the landscape like a showman. 'See the glacier at sea level frozen hard though it's nearly summer! What do you say to that?' He eyed us expectantly and waited. 'Well?'

The air had become noticeably colder and Bernard answered by shivering, or pretending to. 'Dante was taken to visit Hell and found it ice-cold. This must be just such a place!'

'If that makes me Virgil, I thank you for the compliment,' said Gonzalo laughing and making a mock bow.

'It gives me a shrinking feeling, both physically and emotionally. It's like a punishment.'

'Your Latin temperament,' I suggested jovially. 'But the Gospels say Hell is blazing hot.'

Gonzalo wondered whether there might be two Hells, one for the Latin, the other for the Northern mentality.

'Maybe,' conceded Bernard, 'but the main torments are surely spiritual: feeling yourself alien, not belonging where you should belong.'

'Perhaps Hell has no inmates: that's what some saints have claimed,' I said.

'But a purposeless Hell would be a contradiction in terms!'

'You think so? For me, it is devilishly appropriate.' Gonzalo turned to me, looking for my reaction.

'I don't want to sound churlish, but what I see is a vast no-go area. All razor-sharp ridges and crevasses like so many tombs. Hostile, repulsive and useless to man and beast.'

'You are wrong, my friend!' exclaimed Gonzalo, eagerly taking up the challenge. 'Useless *el glaciar* is not! This and all his hundreds of brother glaciers are essential pieces in the make-up of this country. Let me explain. First, our glacier's birth certificate: his parents, the Andes, lie in a belt of prevailing easterly winds. These winds come laden with moisture which falls as snow on the windward side of the mountains.

'You see the brilliant white of the snow in the distance. This glacier results from all that watery load dropping as snowflakes, soft as down and ninety per cent air. Under the weight of more snow, the flakes are squashed into dense grains. Pressure builds up and the ice grains recrystallize. Now the frozen grains cement together. What was once snowflake becomes rock.' So saying, Gonzalo brought out a geologist's hammer from his pocket, knelt down and struck the glacier surface hard.

'*Mira!*' Gonzalo glowed. 'Not a dent. It has the same structure as crystalline rock like marble, but naturally it melts at a much lower temperature.' He described how what we saw before us had once been frozen snow which had built up on the summit. Gravity had it tumbling down the nearest slope, wrenching and gouging out rock in its path, sculpting a new face on the mountain. I imagined the glacier clawing up into its maw all the plants and other organic debris in its way.

'The difference between radioactive carbon in the trapped plants and carbon normally found in living plants tells us the glacier's age. This one is 12,000 years old.'

'Twice older than Khufu's Pyramid,' I murmured.

'But this is all nature's work!' Gonzalo dismissed me with a wave. 'The pressure of overlying ice liquefies the lowest level so the glacier skates slowly to sea level.' He paused for effect. 'It is sliding down at the rate our toenails grow: four centimetres a year.'

Bernard seemed doubtful. 'So you come each year with a tape measure?'

'Yes, accompanied by six handmaidens who perform ritual dances to placate the monster.' Gonzalo became sardonic to cover his irritation, then resumed his thread, 'Further snowfalls are forever replenishing the ice that melts away.'

'All right, so it moves,' I intervened stubbornly. 'But that doesn't alter the fact that it's a repellent blot on the landscape.'

'Archie, you must guard against hidden preconceptions! I suspect you're harbouring a secret wish for Chile to be as green and pretty as Sussex. That's trivializing a serious subject.'

I could not help myself coming back on Gonzalo, so I turned to Bernard. 'Do you see anything trivial in aesthetics? Jesus openly admired the lilies of the field.'

Bernard would not play along. 'But He held aesthetic sense in check when curing lepers.'

'Oh, very well. I'll listen.'

Gonzalo was only too pleased to go on. 'This kind of ice holds important clues about the Earth. Scientists in Antarctica and Greenland have sunk bores two kilometres deep into solid ice and brought up ice cores.' He turned to Bernard, 'You're our expert on minutiae. I'm not saying you're small-minded but you at least will appreciate these bores which are not boring.' Gonzalo's puns were touchingly laboured.

He went on to explain that each ice core is layered and, when analysed using mass spectrometry, oxygen in the ice shows tiny variations. Ordinary oxygen has 16 electrically charged particles called ions; there is also heavy oxygen containing 18 ions. During a cold period, the sea is enriched in oxygen-18 because oxygen-16 is preferentially evaporated and then gets trapped in glacial ice after it precipitates. A high ratio of oxygen-18 is evidence of a relatively warm period. These tiny fluctuations show the age of the ice, just like the rings on a tree trunk.

'We now have a record of the Earth's climate for the last 160,000 years. Cooling periods last around 80,000 years, alternating with shorter warming periods. The last cool period ended 12,000 years ago and our present warm period may continue for another 8,000 years.'

I felt irritated: it was all a bit too pat. 'The Etruscans foretold events by inspecting an ox's liver, with each part matched to a section of the sky. Are your forecasts really any more reliable?'

'On the evidence, yes. And don't be hard on the Etruscans. They understood that sky and weather shape our life on Earth because they form part of one connected whole.'

According to Bernard, climate change determined the distribution and behaviour of animals more than the struggle for food. 'The last cooling period left North Africa fertile and green, that's why Rome could get so many lions for the arena and Hannibal had elephants to frighten the legions.'

Gonzalo returned to defend the honour of the glacier. 'Now for this glacier's usefulness,' he said pointedly, turning to me. 'Our warming atmosphere has been melting more and more snow, so sea levels go up. Think of a glacier as a reservoir of moisture held in place by bonded crystals. If all the glaciers melted, imagine the catastrophe! Coastal waters would rise and Puerto Natales' wooden houses would drown like shipwrecks.' Warming to his theme, Gonzalo explained that glaciers proved their usefulness to man by reflecting sunshine away from Earth, so helping to reduce temperature.

We were struck by his earnestness. With no hint of irony, Bernard responded. 'You've conjured up one of those fairy-tale dragons with a heart of gold. Everyone runs in fear but the dragon just wants to be loved. We'll do our best to love it, eh Archie?'

Further up, the frozen surface peaked in sharp ridges. When Bernard said he wished to examine their structure, Gonzalo readily offered to show him a way up the scree bordering the glacier's southern flank. I preferred to return to the dinghy to look more closely at the glacier's outfall. We agreed a rendez-vous.

Cautiously, I edged my way down, zigzagging along the scree leading to the water. Here the glacier's end was hidden by a promontory. The distance was short and I asked the boatman not to use the outboard. He rowed the dinghy southwards with slow strong strokes, then swung round the headland, putting the sun behind us.

Directly ahead we could see what looked like a giant meringue topped with whipped cream which, as we paddled on, was transformed into something more like a baroque cupola, all cumulus clouds and cherubs. Closer still and another vision hit us, as of an edifice rising from the water built of cyclopean ice-blocks, some squared, others serrated and all jammed together in a freezing *rigor mortis*. Here the glacier's meltwater was hurling itself over the cliff in an unending suicide while simultaneously building itself a high mausoleum which gleamed like white marble.

The hold on me exerted by the convulsive turmoil before my eyes began to ease as our boat edged closer to the ice façade and I spotted a gently curving arch leading into an ice cavern. I asked the boatman to make for it but, well short of the arch, he refused to go further, saying a strong current might lock us in. He backpaddled and steadied the boat safely out of reach of the current yet facing the cavern, perhaps thirty metres away.

25

Within the cavern rose a free-standing block of ice which was partly hollowed out. From its centre streamed a blue light, steady and intense as starlight but without flicker and blue in colour, purest aquamarine blue. Where other light illuminates, this instead drew the eye to itself and held it.

Once before I had encountered a strange light: the nervous, jumpy glow of phosphorescence on breaking water. This light was quite different: self-contained and self-sustaining. How could it hold its own against packed ice? And why was it blue? Think it out, I urged myself. Blue light belongs to the sky and the sea is blue when reflecting the sky. Therefore this light, which was hidden from the sky, must be blue in and by itself. This idea added to the fascination I felt, quickening my heartbeat and setting me musing. If ice preserves the past, could this light not belong to an earlier age? To the most distant age of all? Why not?

Might this be pristine matter with a heartbeat of light? Yet it was immaterial, not of our Earth. Older still and sky blue. Before Day One, before sun and moon, obedient to the *fiat lux*, original blue light, light that would scatter nothingness and become the heavens, Heaven itself. Yet not beyond our reach. For it would sometimes come down to us as when, on a mountain apart in Palestine, it lit the clothing of three human forms so that they appeared transfigured. And now in this secret cavern the light shone as from a sanctuary lamp. Why? To remind us, perhaps, that perfection does exist – here and perhaps also hereafter.

I was aware of myself wondering and guessing, but also that I was seated uncomfortably in a boat, bobbing in backwash from the meltfall. I had not been fantasizing.

The boatman looked at his watch: our time was up. He steered away from the cavern and we headed for our meeting place. Gonzalo and Bernard climbed aboard, the motor was coaxed to turn and, once more, we cleared the placid surface.

I sensed I was being a bore but I had an urgent need to express what I had felt so deeply. Gonzalo made no comment, but Bernard showed interest. 'It is possible the movement of the boat produced a narcotic effect,' he ventured.

'No. There was nothing hazy or blurred about my vision. It was intense and clear. Can you explain it?'

'Perhaps not,' said Gonzalo with fake modesty, 'but I can clarify.' He said that the mysterious light would originally have been white. Within the berg, it interacted with ice crystals which scattered its whiteness and made it more energetic, with a shorter wavelength. On passing through the cornea, this light was bent and focused by the lens and then arrived at the retina. Photomultiplier cells vastly increased the energy in the light and receptor cones sensitive to wavelengths identified and marked its colour as blue. Then it was returned to the left side of the retina. Images on the left side pass via the optic nerve to the left brain hemisphere which acts as a storehouse of emotional memory.

'Here,' he said, patting his head, 'your blue light elicited the associations you describe. Enriched with these and unmonitored by the critical scrutiny which occurs in the right brain hemisphere, the light passed to your visual cortex where, for the first time, you actually saw blue light, plus an invisible *cortège* of past emotions.'

'So that's why I felt so elated!'

'It may be that love at first sight happens the same way. What the French call *le coup de foudre*.' He paused, then added, 'Knowing the physiological basis does not mean you destroy the wonder. For me, it adds a new kind of wonder but maybe it seems more prosaic to you.'

'I see now that I cannot truly share my experience – I cannot share this supernatural feeling.' It was frustrating.

Under Gonzalo's direction, our boatman entered a wider, zigzag waterway through which coursed a strong current. The view was now dominated by the three immense towers, granite outcrops topping the mountains beneath, the colour of a tortoiseshell cat, with the sun's rays burnishing them orange. From a distance, one might have taken them for the spires of a Romanesque church or else spaceships ready for launching. Though their flanks were pitted, only the most reckless mountaineer would dream of climbing them, for their summits are points atop sheer walls.

Why *Torres del Paine*? I wondered. The first Spanish settlers did not come this far south: it was often Englishmen from ships like the *Beagle* who charted and mapped. With Gonzalo admitting his ignorance about how they came to be named, I suggested that he rechristen them *Torres de la Trinidad*. He looked surprised, thought a moment, then shook his head. 'The Trinity are three in one. This trio is one in three!'

Minutes later we landed on a platform made of planks. From there we crossed a fast-flowing river, making our way over a shaky bridge to find ourselves with a view of a wide valley. Grassland and evergreen trees extended into the distance. The country was evidently fertile since Gonzalo remarked that Chilean deer might be seen. Bernard took out his binoculars and scanned the scene. Minutes later he announced, 'A large bird resembling a cassowary.'

'Good,' said Gonzalo. 'That will be the *ñandú*, Chile's version of the ostrich. The male incubates the eggs and raises the chicks.'

After walking into the landscape for a short while, the valley opened up into shelving hills rising up to the Andes, their peaks bare of snow for it was summer. On the shelves between valley and mountains glistened several beautiful lakes, some aquamarine, one white, another pale green. Gonzalo described that the snow melt and rain that fed the lakes evidenced the minerals of each mountain to which it was subject.

Gonzalo spread his arms towards the spectacle before us. 'Everything you see here and further on for many kilometres is national park. There's an eleven-day circuit for back-packers, no houses except for a scattering of woodsmen's cabins. This is virgin territory. Its beauty and its animals are protected by the State.'

We retraced our route to the bridge and back to the landing place where our boatman was waiting. Twenty minutes later we were in Puerto Natales.

Having retrieved our belongings from the shipping office, we found a fish restaurant facing the sea. There we ordered a local speciality, the *centolla* which looks like a reddish eight-pointed starfish but is in fact a spider crab with flesh akin to a lobster's. It has the further advantage that the shell is easily removed from the claws. We savoured the meringue with apricot jam while Gonzalo went off to book places on the afternoon bus to Punta Arenas.

I had warmed to Bernard though I still knew little about him. Over coffee I asked him about his field of medicine. He explained that he headed a team researching the treatment of leukaemia. One day a week, he monitored six children receiving bone marrow transplants under his care. He did not want research to distance him from his chosen vocation of healing the sick.

'I want to know how you imagine my laboratory, Archie.'

'Very secret, highly hush-hush. Magnetic card to open two sets of doors. Sterilized white gown and masks. Row upon row of expensive instruments. A private language of numbers and neologisms. Now that you possess the genome, you can read each of us like a book, you can tell us our strengths and failings, what we'll transmit to our children and when our ageing gene

29

is timed to finish us off. You can read the book of life so you have more power than any priesthood or clutch of soothsayers ever dreamed of.'

Bernard laughed aloud. 'Just as I thought – newspaper fantasy. Our lab is very small, just enough for myself and three assistants. We experiment on small animals, usually mice, which have the same genome as you and me. I am completely dependent on my very expensive little electromicroscope and the mixers that identify molecules invisible to the naked eye. Maybe one appears out of the ordinary but, before I can be sure, I must test many related molecules, a week of trial and error.

'When I've finished my day's work I write about anything useful I've found for the medical journals. Mostly they are in English and my wife helps me translate my findings because I've never truly mastered English. Actually the whole process makes me feel quite small.'

That's why he grows a moustache, I said to myself, to make himself feel less small. 'Surely you don't feel small all the time?' I quizzed him.

'When I discover something that looks important I get grand ideas. I lift up my head and get ready to celebrate with a bottle of champagne. But when I leave the lab and drive home through all the traffic, I realise none of my fellow microbiologists will believe what I've found.'

'Why ever not?'

'Because what I've found is strong evidence that each human is a uniquely complex creature whom only a Creator could have made.'

Gonzalo rejoined us. He had bought tickets for the three o'clock departure and had been advised we should instal ourselves early to secure good seats near the front. This we did, only to find that no more than three local passengers joined us, plus the ticket collector who entered into a long conversation with the driver without ever asking to see our tickets. We left on time and were soon making good speed on a straight macadam road. Every few kilometres, a little Chinese-style kiosk decorated in coloured glazed tiles marked the entrance to one of the many huge estates called *estancias*, providing shelter for those awaiting the occasional bus. Of the *estancias* we could see no sign: they were presumably set too far back from the road. More astonishing was the absence of fencing and livestock.

As our bus continued south without stopping at any of the kiosks, either to drop off a passenger or pick up another, the land on both sides of the road became less and less productive. The grass was dry and colourless, uncropped and unkempt. I found this depressing but worse was to come. More frequent than kiosks were the white skeletons of what had been trees looking like the bones of prehistoric beasts. There was no living tree to be seen. What had not been cut down for fuel had been felled by the deadly Patagonian wind blowing in from the Pacific. The sight of these skeletons on the already desert-like land gave the place the air of a vast cemetery and struck me as tragic.

What had happened? Looking as usual on the bright side, Gonzalo proceeded to explain. In 1877 an English trader had brought a flock of sheep from the Falklands to one of Chile's Patagonian islands. The experiment proved a success and soon other entrepreneurs followed. Farm administrators arrived from Britain, mainly Welsh and Scottish, and farm hands were brought in from the overcrowded holdings on Chiloé. The *estancias* we were passing were highly profitable until the Great Depression of the 1930s. Thereafter competition from Australia, New Zealand and Canada squeezed Chile from the major world markets and so the entrepreneurs went home, leaving their estates to disintegrate slowly and their big houses to collapse. The trees they had planted were done for by the wind or by peons.

Gonzalo left his seat to talk to our driver, asking him to stop briefly at the next kiosk. We got out to stretch our legs and Gonzalo directed our attention to the long driveway cutting across the run-down land. 'Hidden away down there is Estancia San Gregorio. It was built in 1878 and belonged to the most famous farming entrepreneur, Don José Menendez. His sheep farm extended to 90,000 hectares, with a huge mansion, shops and bars for the labour force, as well as a chapel and a theatre for the owner and his family. The fall in world prices forced them to reduce the *estancia* and cut down the number of sheep but the house is still in private hands.'

Another stop, a second chance to stretch our legs. Bernard and I got out; Gonzalo stayed put, talking into his mobile to check our overnight booking in Punta Arenas. There was no kiosk here. Instead we found a tall thin mast of gleaming metal. Could it be a radio transmitter? It seemed oddly situated, with no houses in sight and it had a horizontal metal curlicue attached to the point. The curlicue was carefully fashioned, about a forearm in length, its convolutions in direct contrast to the smoothness of the mast.

Bernard rejected my suggestion that it was for radio transmission and declared the important part was the curlicue, the pole merely serving as support.

'But why so high?' I queried. 'Why make it difficult for the spectator to see?'

Bernard offered another explanation. On a visit to Spain, he'd been struck by contemporary Spanish sculpture, very often abstracts in sheet metal. He remembered one such statue in Fuengirola in honour of the Archangel Gabriel, to whom the town was dedicated. Yet how unlikely, I felt, that this remote part of Chile would have much to do with Spanish sculptors. Perhaps, rather, school children were taught that the Greeks had a god of the wind called Aeolus, who released his great gusts from a volcanic island north of Sicily: if they wanted a statue of the wind, they would have depicted it as a god.

The bus driver joined us and pointed to an official notice fixed to the ground which we had missed. Indeed it read *Statue to the Wind.* 'On top is a lady's windswept hair,' he indicated.

I considered this carefully. 'The statue is a plea to the wind god to cease being so destructive.'

Bernard had a different idea. 'Suppose the notice is mistaken. Perhaps it should read "Statue *of* the Wind", a warning uttered by a disillusioned settler who tried farming here and found it impossible.'

'Maybe. Or perhaps it's intended as an enigma, like the Sphinx. For centuries men have been going to Giza with difficult queries to solve and the Sphinx is reckoned to have given satisfactory answers. What question shall we put to the wind? And will it give a satisfactory answer?'

We returned to the bus. Twenty minutes later, I was still absorbed in thinking about the wind statue and hardly noticed when street lights appeared. Gonzalo announced our arrival in Punta Arenas.

CHAPTER FOUR

Antarctic Tribes

The habitable Antarctic gets twenty hours of daylight in the summer and the sunshine woke us early. We walked down to the docks and the port with its outlet to the Atlantic by way of the Magellan Strait, named after Portugal's epic navigator who first mapped it. Punta Arenas is sheltered from both the Pacific and Atlantic but not from the gusts blowing in off the icy waters of the strait. Since the sixteenth century, the port has offered a halfway haven for ships trading between East and West, North and South.

Gonzalo put the scene into perspective, explaining that what we could see ten kilometres to the east was the Isla Grande de Tierra del Fuego, so named by Ferdinand Magellan because he saw smoke rising from native campfires. The island is mostly mountainous and shared between Chile and Argentina 70 to 30 per cent respectively, a chronic source of dispute. 'Our neighbour Argentina, four times our size and as rich in land as we are poor, is often threatening us. Until recently, all her governments have been military and aggressive. Often they have crossed the difficult-to-define frontier stretching along 6,000 kilometres of the Andes.'

Bernard intervened politely. 'After Hitler fell, wasn't it the Argentine government that invited top Nazis to come and live in Buenos Aires?'

'Alas yes! They showed their aggressive side when they took the Falkland Islands.' Turning to me, he cried, 'They forced your country to fight an uphill war and many brave lives were lost. I'm proud to say Chile gave Britain valued moral support.'

Gonzalo mentioned an earlier dispute with Argentina in 1978. Having roused my curiosity, he then said it would take too long to explain. That evening, I pressed him again and he related a remarkable story. Shortly before Christmas 1978, Argentina decided to show its strength by occupying three small islands lying close to Fuego's southern coast. The islands had never been mentioned when Fuego was partitioned so now they were contested. The United States offered to decide the affair even-handedly but any suggestion of compromise was refused by Argentina which announced an ultimatum. Unless Chile allowed the occupation, there would be war. Argentina had already made an agreement with Bolivia, Chile's northern neighbour, simultaneously to attack Chile's northern port Arica, and make it a free outlet for Bolivia's timber exports.

Equipped with only a small army, Chile would not have been able to defend itself against full-scale attack from north and south. The Chilean foreign minister decided to appeal to the Vatican for arbitration and, hopefully, a settlement. But Pope Paul VI happened to be seriously ill and died soon after. The minister then privately approached his successor, John Paul, only to learn that he died in his sleep less than a month after becoming Pope.

Time was running out. The Chilean foreign minister continued his pressure on the Vatican. The new Pope, John Paul II, had displayed a genius for arbitration when freeing his country from the Kremlin's grip at the time of the Gdansk shipyard strike. The Pope agreed to intervene and instructed the minister to meet his representative secretly in Hong Kong. As a result of their discussions, the Pope warned Argentina that, unless she backed off, and agreed to arbitration, she would invite the condemnation of Rome and the rest of the world. Argentina complied; under papal supervision, the agreement concluded in 1984 was accepted by both countries.

Next day we breakfasted on the *plaza* and now it was my turn to share knowledge. I asked Gonzalo and Bernard whether they cared to hear about my research into the life of Charles Darwin. They agreed that Darwin was a key figure in the fields of geology and anthropology and were keen to learn about my findings.

I began my story in 1833, the year England first occupied the Falkland Islands. Darwin, on board the *Beagle*, a naval ship charting the seas of South America, arrived off Fuego. He was not interested in indigenous peoples; his energies were devoted to shooting rare unfamiliar birds and sending their annotated remains back to London, as evidence that he was more than just an amateur naturalist. In Chile alone he shot seventy different species.

Setting foot in Fuego, he encountered a group of natives and described them in his *Journal*: 'I never saw such miserable creatures, stunted in their growth, their hideous faces bedaubed with white paint and quite naked… Their red skins filthy and greasy, their voices discordant, their gesticulation violent and without any dignity. Viewing such men, one can hardly believe that they are fellow creatures placed in the same world.'

What Darwin doesn't say in his *Journal* is that there were three Fuegians on board the *Beagle* dressed like Europeans and able to speak English. On a previous voyage, FitzRoy, the *Beagle*'s captain, had taken three Fuegian men and one woman to England and arranged for them to be well cared for. Able and eager, they soon understood the language and spoke it a little. One of them died in London from infectious disease and now the others, Jemmy Button, York Minster and Fuegia

Basket, were being repatriated. The passengers had a sense of humour and were popular with the crew. Darwin must have seen them and probably also spoke with them.

FitzRoy was a true humanitarian. He had studied his three Fuegians closely and was convinced that it would only be fair to return them to their native land; he believed that they had become sufficiently civilized to retain their new lifestyle and perhaps teach it to others. So Jemmy, York and Fuegia were rowed ashore in Wollaston Bay, and the *Beagle* set sail through the Magellan Strait for Argentina and Uruguay.

A year later, the *Beagle* began its homeward voyage to England, having returned to Fuego. The crew landed at Ponsonby Sound and set up camp, close to where Jemmy Button had made his home after leaving FitzRoy. Soon after the crew had installed themselves, canoes approached in which some of the occupants could be seen anxiously scrubbing white paint from their faces. One looked familiar: it was Jemmy.

Darwin found him thin, pale and with no clothes save for a bit of blanket around his waist; his hair hung down his shoulders. It seemed that he was ashamed of himself in front of his old friends. He looked up and raised his hand, 'as a sailor touches his hat.' A pathetic salute. FitzRoy bundled him on board and clothed him, ready for dinner at the Captain's table. He used knife and fork correctly and, speaking as much English as ever, told Darwin and FitzRoy of his companions' behaviour. York Minster had persuaded him to come back to his own country deep in the interior. There, one night, while he slept, York and Fuegia had fled with all his possessions, leaving him as FitzRoy had first found him, naked.

Outside in a canoe, a young and – for a Fuegian – beautiful squaw was weeping. She was pregnant and said to be Jemmy's wife. Only his reappearance on deck soothed her. The next day after breakfast, Jemmy bade them goodbye. He had 'not the least wish to return to England'. He was too contented with 'plenty fruits, plenty birdies', and 'ten guanaco in snow time'. For the crew, he left a pair of fine otter skins, arrows for FitzRoy and 'two spearheads for Mr Darwin'. He had made them himself. The ship got underway while he was still on board, prompting more sobbing from his squaw. He quickly dropped into his canoe and dried her tears.

In 1859, twenty-five years after that moving farewell, Darwin published his *On the Origin of Species* in which he claimed as scientific truth that man was descended by natural selection from the same stock as simians. All England was astonished, shaken and divided into two camps: the Darwinians as against those who claimed that man was created by God. It was to prove a chasm that would remain unbridged for one hundred and fifty years.

In a famous debate held in London, FitzRoy cited his first-hand evidence of the Fuegians based on his knowledge of them as well as accounts given of their capabilities by European settlers. Fuegians employed on sheep farms learned Spanish and showed remarkably retentive memory. After listening to two pages of a book read to them, they could recite the whole back word-perfect. It was found that the Fuegian language had a vocabulary of no less than 30,000 words while basic English comprises 1,000 words.

Not surprisingly, FitzRoy publicly opposed Darwin's view of man as an improved simian. But Darwin had friends in high places, whereas FitzRoy was just a former naval officer and, instead of citing Jemmy Button's speedy adoption of civilized behaviour and manners, he stood by his first description of the Fuegians as he remembered it.

'The Fuegians had tousled hair, gesticulated excitedly, pulled grotesque faces, and none had even a stitch of clothing.' It was this last trait that weighed with upper-class Englishmen.

Victoria was a much-loved Queen and puritan attitudes were *de rigueur*. If the Fuegians lived out their lives naked as monkeys and apes, then clearly Darwin's theory – it was no more than a theory – of natural selection, later amplified in another book *The Descent of Man*, must be implicitly endorsed, however offensive to Christians.

Gonzalo was clearly pleased to learn more about Captain FitzRoy who had made himself liked on his two voyages, thanks to his Samaritan attitude to Fuegians, in marked contrast to that of the majority of Europeans.

Bernard showed little interest. 'In France, Darwin's name is not taken seriously. Most scientists believe with Lamarck that we transmit physical and mental characteristics to our children, who may or may not modify them.' Then, turning to Gonzalo, 'All I observe here are seals and sea lions, both very boring. Not even a square-headed sperm whale. Where are your indigenous animals? Where are your penguins?'

Gonzalo sympathized but said we had only limited time. 'It's a three-hour drive to our *pinguineros*. Our Magellanic penguins are breeding this season, living in burrows dug into the sandy shoreline. Probably you wouldn't see them. Perhaps you would like to visit the enormous Milodon Cave, the hideout of a gigantic sloth?' Bernard declared himself interested in the sloth as a rare South American species but he had never heard of a giant sloth.

A car and a driver were found to take us to the cave. The car was a two-year-old Toyota, its coachwork already marred by the gusty salt wind. Gonzalo reported that it had come by ship direct from Japan, closer than North America. 'Nearly all heavy goods here are brought in across the Pacific, making them very expensive. Cement and strong timber for building, bulk foods like rice and flour, the latest equipment for the hospitals, you name it, it has to come by sea. Even from Santiago, more than

5,000 kilometres away and with no continuous land route. The post comes from Santiago by plane, along with all the newspapers and magazines. There's a small airport just north of the town. Supplying the Magallanes region puts a heavy strain on the economy. Part of the price for inheriting an impoverished but fascinating land.'

The Milodon Cave proved to be enormous in height and depth, extending inward into total darkness: as eerie a cave as I had ever seen. It was discovered a hundred years ago and on its floor was found a large piece of the occupant's hairy pelt along with the skull of a large mammal, a claw and a human thigh bone. Comparison with similar bones of other prehistoric mammals made it possible to identify the cave occupant as a giant ground sloth, a species endemic to South America. Carbon dating of the hairy skin proved that it had lived around 8,000 BC. The human thigh bone suggested it was a man-eater.

Near the cave entrance was a life-size statue of the giant sloth. The beast stood erect on its hind legs, claw arms extended threateningly, head thrust forward, jaws ready to snap. The model created a good approximation of the terror it would have inspired in prehistoric man.

The notion of a giant man-eating sloth set me thinking. 'A sloth in French is a *paresseux* which is also the adjective for lazy. What is the Spanish?'

'*Perezoso*, also meaning lazy,' replied Gonzalo.

'If an animal is defined in that way, it shows what is in fact true: its chief characteristic is laziness, which is extremely rare in the animal kingdom.' I went on thinking aloud, 'Why does the sloth make its home in the jungle, never in caves? Because it spends most of each day in the foliage of strong trees.' I recalled what I knew about sloths, that they live near the tops of trees in hammocks they construct out of branches: they lift their strong forearms above the head to grip a stout branch and curl their toes around a lower branch, so making the hammock safe. The animal's habits are unadventurous and unaggressive. Much of its diet is vegetarian. Its legs are poorly developed whereas the arms are muscular to take the weight of its supine body. 'I'm not convinced it was man-eating. One human thigh bone proves nothing. It could have belonged to a human hunter.'

Gonzalo objected. 'The statue was commissioned by the Chilean expert on sloths.'

'Then the sculptor let his imagination run away with him. It's exaggerated and completely misleading!'

'You'll see a strip of the sloth's skin and a heap of its droppings at the Regional Museum. Then you may change your mind,' pronounced Gonzalo loftily.

The car jogged us back to Punta Arenas. In a café on the plaza we ate a light lunch washed down by excellent Chilean beer. Then we took a long walk away from the port. Not far from the town cemetery, we came to the Church of Our Lady of Succour belonging to the Order of Salesians founded by St Francis de Sales and known for its fine schools. Next to it stands the Salesian Regional Museum, one of the best in South America. We approached the entrance only to find that it was 'closed for redecoration'.

'What local museum isn't closed for repairs or staff shortages?' asked Gonzalo rhetorically. Undismayed, he inquired after the director's address and went to find him. Ten minutes later, he reappeared with the man who not only unlocked the door for us but also seemed honoured to have been asked.

What was it about Gonzalo? On board the *Puerto Eden*, the captain knew him by name and gave him the run of the bridge. The manager at our hotel treated us as VIPs. Was Gonzalo himself our pass-key? I remembered that his letter inviting me to Chile was written on paper headed *Commissariat for National*

Resources. He was in a position to advise the Government about economic development. Couple that with the fact that, as a university student, he had come out against General Pinochet, led a group of student protesters, become a near-hero and suffered imprisonment and exile. Would that not make him honoured by Chilean patriots of all ages?

Gonzalo's special combination of qualifications meant we could now admire the museum's exhibits. We went to look at the display case with the large pelt said to belong to the giant sloth. Bernard crouched down to examine it methodically for a full five minutes. 'The mammal with skin which resembles this most closely is the grizzly bear. But such bears belong to Canada and Alaska.'

Gonzalo next led us to the museum's main display of dioramas. 'For convenience we've been talking about Fuegians,' he explained. In fact there were three different native tribes. The dioramas showed how they lived and what they ate using three-dimensional models. The Alcalufe lived out their lives huddled in small wooden boats, diving for shellfish and hunting seals and sea lions. A few were taken in and clothed by philanthropic Europeans but by and large they were left alone. The Europeans in Punta Arenas overfished their waters and obliged the Alcalufe to move far to the north. Their surviving descendants live in the islets of Puerto Eden. These were the tribespeople posing stiffly in Gonzalo's old photograph.

The next diorama was devoted to the Ona tribe which hunted *guanaco* – a smaller relative of the llama – on the northern plains of Tierra del Fuego. European settlers imported flocks of sheep to replace the guanaco and the Ona retaliated by hunting the sheep with bows and arrows. The European reaction was massacre and the Ona tribe was wiped out in the early 1900s.

We turned to the Yaghane who were still to be found in large numbers, concentrated in the icy forested islands south of the

Beagle Channel. 'They go about mainly naked,' pronounced Gonzalo. 'They're an intelligent people but fight among themselves and can behave cruelly when threatened.'

I recalled that the exotic passengers on board the Beagle were Yaghane. We had already encountered the contrasting views of them given by Darwin and FitzRoy.

'By the early 1900s, it looked as though the settlers were preparing to kill all the *Indios*, just as the Argentinians had already done in their part of Tierra del Fuego. What could the Government do to prevent it, 3,200 kilometres away and with no aeroplanes yet to bridge the gap?' Gonzalo turned to Bernard. 'Does the year 1906 in France mean anything to you?'

Bernard prepared his reply carefully. He explained how, during the whole nineteenth century, French education had been run by the Catholic church and had enjoyed a high reputation. But in 1900, the politician Jules Ferry launched a campaign to exclude the teaching of Christianity from schools and, in 1906, a law was passed defining France as *laïque*, an ambiguous term equivalent to 'secular'. With no chance of putting their case before the courts, 30,000 men and women from the Catholic teaching orders were expelled from France forever. Their schools and property were made over to the State. 'It was the most spiritually devastating year in our history since 1789,' he concluded.

Gonzalo took up the story. The most numerous and esteemed of the teaching Orders was the Salesian which had been founded in France three centuries earlier. A few of its members found work in Spain and Italy, but others had to look overseas. 'One group came to Chile, built this presbytery where we are now and set about trying to save Fuegians from the settlers.' The Salesians did not know how to deal with a backward people with no interest in improving their way of life. Scrubbing their faces free of white paint and teaching them basic Spanish infringed their identity. Each tribe looked upon its language to distinguish its identity. So the Salesians set about learning the native languages, a difficult time-consuming task. This gradually won the tribespeople's confidence and only then did the Salesians start missionary work amongst those who seemed ready for it. They set up refuges for Fuegians away from sheep farms, in places without European settlers. One group was settled in the beautiful Isla Dawson.

'When they were grouped together – men, women and children – they could not be left naked without exciting sexual appetite, rivalry and hatred. So the Salesians ordered clothing from Europe and the Fuegians accepted it without fuss. We are proud of the Salesians. They saved the Fuegians from extinction.'

Gonzalo turned away from the dioramas to view the wooden canoes, spears, bows and arrows which were lined up in cases. 'Sadly there was a twist to this saga. In 1918 a new Black Death hit Europe. Influenza killed a million people.'

Bernard looked sombre. 'Did ships carry the germ to Chile?'

'Yes, and it killed 500 Fuegians on the Isla Dawson. Settlers blamed their deaths on the clothing to which they were unaccustomed. But that is absolute nonsense! Chile still offers sympathy and practical help to her minorities – not just to her backward people, but also to immigrants whose lives have been shattered by war. There are many here from Eastern Europe.'

Gonzalo announced that he had an appointment with the *alcade*, the mayor, and would leave us to our own devices. Bernard opted to go to the cathedral on the main square while I walked off in the opposite direction towards the port. I found the Harbour Master in his office. He was a smartly turned out former naval officer in his fifties, wearing a yachtsman's cap and speaking fluent English, essential for dealing with cosmopolitan crews. I started by asking what had happened to the port after the Panama Canal pinched most of its traffic.

'Very difficult times, right through to the Great Depression when we lost our wool exports to Australia and New Zealand. But Punta Arenas fought back. With Argentina breathing down our necks, we were harbouring Chile's fleet of small warships. Then we decided to declare Punta Arenas a duty-free port. This attracted ships rounding Cape Horn. We have a modern workshop for repairing engine failure and even a hotel equipped with jacuzzis. It's much in demand after the icy cold of the Straits. Now Punta Arenas is no longer the End of the World. It's the starting point for adventurers from all over.'

'Sailing yachts single-handed round the Cape?' I ventured.

'Better than that, and considerably less dangerous. This is the gateway to the Antarctic. They come to see what they've talked about at home. Global warming. They see iceberg after iceberg, each a glacier honed by furious winds, drifting north and slowly melting. These floating mountains are mysterious and unforgettable.' After such a response I felt that any further question would be banal. I thanked my helpful informant and took my leave.

On the waterfront I heard seamen exchanging stories about foreigners from cruise ships who came ashore for an hour or two before setting off for Antarctica. Back at the hotel, I found Bernard who had gone down to the fishing harbour to talk to the men and see what they were catching. He told me that Chile shared the world problem of over-fishing. 'To the warm waters of the Pacific, add the cold Humbolt Current and all that's best in firm-fleshed fish is within range of your nets,' he explained. The fish can be caught but it may not be sold. Many of the fishermen's little boats lay upturned on the shore while their owners sat idly by. Yet they had not complained to

Bernard: they received compensation from the town authorities for not overfishing.

Bernard described his visit to the cathedral, built around 1900 and still in good repair. He had got talking to one of the ladies arranging flowers on the high altar. She told him that the Yugoslav arrivals were more regular church-goers than the Chileans and were more engaged in parish activities. Involvement gave them a sense of being home.

When Gonzalo joined us for dinner, he asked for our views on Punta Arenas. 'Always new difficulties alternating with brave new solutions. That's Chile!' He volunteered another example of Chilean resourcefulness. In 1945, prospecting for oil began in several parts of the Magellanes. Oil was discovered, wells were sunk and Punta Arenas expected to do as well as Norway and Britain with offshore oil. But fifteen years later, the oil ran dry. Natural gas reserves were found but Chile lacked the financial resources to extract and refine it. No foreign investor appeared interested in the icy town. After twenty years, Chile finally found a Canadian company willing to risk its money. Now Punta Arenas boasted one of the largest and most efficient methanol plants in the world.

We chatted about Chile's economic progress but Gonzalo soon cut us short. 'Early tomorrow morning we take the plane to Santiago. You will see other difficulties and other solutions!' he promised.

CHAPTER FIVE

A City that Trembles

On the flight to Santiago Bernard and I sat next to each other, with Gonzalo behind us peering through his window. After gaining height, our plane levelled out and Gonzalo commented on the landscape beneath. 'Chile's Lake District. Just imagine the massive glaciers tumbling from the High Andes down to ground level until they melt. The larger lakes are like Annecy and Windermere, fine for sailing or bathing, weather permitting.'

The settlers who came here were not Spanish but German, he explained. From 1885 to 1910 they came *en masse* bringing their arts, crafts, foundries and capacity for hard work. They prospered whilst still retaining their German dress, folklore and concertina music. Many went into business with Chileans to rear wild salmon in the lakes.

Gonzalo adopted a solemn tone as he declared, 'the land between the Lakes is fertile and that's where we grow most of our fruit and grapes. There's very little of it, but it's the one and only part of Chile that's bountiful.'

We landed at Santiago airport on time and were met by Gonzalo's driver, who took us to the city centre. Our host went off to attend meetings, leaving Bernard and me to our own devices. We chose a small-old fashioned hotel near the historic centre of Santiago, with an open-air restaurant on its top floor.

Bernard set off on a short ski-ing trip but I had wanted to spend more time in the capital the better to appreciate the extent of pollution and the earthquake implications of my brief. The friendly porter gave me directions, and a ten-minute walk along tree-lined avenues brought me to a range of smart shops, cafés and banks. From the Plaza de Armas, I walked south to find an immense queue of men and women winding round two blocks. I followed the queue round to its destination, the Municipal Theatre. They were waiting for the box office to open at midday to buy tickets for the evening performance of Verdi's *Traviata*. Posters advertised a series of concerts by the Strasbourg Symphony Orchestra as well as recitals by various Chilean soloists.

Retracing my steps, I entered the eighteenth century cathedral where shoppers were kneeling for brief prayers before adding to the lighted candles in front of St Teresa. The nearby walls were crammed with *ex voto* plaques.

I headed for a vast open space, lined with trees and fountains. Here were numerous free-standing statues of heroes and presidents with European names. There were two grandiose monuments, one a memorial to members of Chile's police force who died trying to control rioters in the hungry years of Allende's presidency. The other took the form of an out-of-date aeroplane and commemorated the brave pilots who flew the postal service between Paris and Santiago. Many of the museums and historic buildings were built by French and Italian architects and this was what lent Santiago its cosmopolitan, European feel. One or two high-rise blocks were the only sign of modernism. Taking a crowded bus, I began to get the feel of the city. From its busy centre, it spread out in all directions, embracing large well-kept parks, middle-class residential suburbs and the tightly clustered adobe and wood dwellings of the poor. A modern, scrupulously clean metro system ran east and west to the capital's upper-class suburb Las Condas where the de luxe hotels are situated.

I had been told it was bad manners to talk to Santaguinos about their earthquakes. For a start, they were no longer termed earthquakes, only tremors. At the first rumble, Santaguinos were drilled to shift a heavy table into the centre of their living rooms, open all the doors and then squeeze under the table till the tremor stops: a very humiliating experience. Then they emerge to find all the pictures on the walls have tilted slightly.

Starting in 1552, three earthquakes have destroyed the beautiful cathedral and devastated the city. The source of Chile's earthquakes lies offshore under the Pacific where the Andean tectonic plate is deeply fissured. If the tectonic plate should buckle some more, then the quakes will become more violent. One Santaguino ready to discuss tremors and quakes was of course Gonzalo. He offered to show me round the only house which had survived repeated earthquakes.

Casa Colorada stands by itself in a small square, striking red-pitched walls enclosing a typical one-floor upper-class home with spacious rooms arranged to convey the atmosphere of a wealthy family home in the eighteenth century when Santiago was prospering. Ladies wore hooped skirts, colourful silk gloves and set off their hair with lace caps while men sported velvet breeches, buckle shoes, gold braid jackets and tricorne hats atop wigs. Murals depicted scenes of family games, outdoor parties and excursions in horse-drawn carriages. Louis XV armchairs emphasized Santiago's debt to Parisian style on the eve of the French Revolution.

'If this was the only house to survive repeated earthquakes, why didn't the government shift the capital far from seismic shocks?'

Gonzalo shrugged. 'They just kept rebuilding on the same site!'

'Wasn't that unwise?'

'This was where Pedro de Valdivia chose to make his capital in 1541. Straight off, he and his 150 conquistadors fought off an attack by a huge force of native warriors. Pride dictates that we remain on the site of that victory.'

We wandered up to the steep hill from which Valdivia had planned his settlement. It was a baroque maze of gardens, fountains and paths, a spot for engaged couples to hold hands and exchange a discreet kiss. Here was a memorial plaque engraved with an extract of a letter sent by Valdivia to the Emperor Charles V five years after the victory, extolling Chile's climate.

On the summit were buildings barred to the public where Chile's geologists keep their early warning systems. We were given a friendly welcome by another of Gonzalo's acquaintances. The man pointed to his seismometer, its pen rolling smoothly along the scroll, sensitive to invisible earth tremors as a barometer is to air pressure. If the pen wavered slightly, an earthquake might hit the coast but, if it fluctuated widely, it meant the Nazca plate had crunched under the Peru-Chile plate and Santiago was in line for destruction. Sirens would warn the four million inhabitants to evacuate tall buildings and head for open spaces.

The man explained how each of Earth's continents and oceans rides on an immense rocky plate. There are fifteen of these, all jostling and gradually moving about. Most are just slabs of ocean floor, but some of the larger ones carry the lighter continents on their backs. In South America, one plate carries the Andes which were formed forty million years ago by pressure from the Nazca plate. This gouged a long and very deep gash one hundred miles offshore known as the Peru-Chile trench. The Nazca plate dives into the trench, then grinds under the Andean plate. 'If the grinding intensifies,' he smiled beatifically, 'Chile's fifty active volcanoes will erupt with an upflow of hot rock from Earth's mantle.'

'What drives the moving plates?' I asked.

'Expert opinion is divided. Probably the heat released inside the Earth by radioactive atoms.'

'Monitoring seismometers must keep you in a state of chronic nervous tension.'

'You can say that again. But to us geologists, earthquakes are also a blessing. Although they occur just below the Earth's surface, the waves of disturbance pass right through the planet, effectively x-raying it. One type of wave can travel only through solids. If the Earth were completely solid, these waves would be picked up by seismometers all over the planet. But in fact seismometers situated exactly opposite an earthquake never pick up this type of wave. Therefore Earth must have a liquid core that absorbs the waves. Probably made of molten iron-nickel.'

'So you know the cause of earthquakes. But what about the man in the street?'

'He believes God allows earthquakes to happen. It's the poor who suffer the worst, either killed outright or left homeless.'

'Could they be rehoused in a safer area?'

'They'd refuse to go. They have their roots here… For all our knowledge, we cannot really help.' He spread his hands: it was a hint that he had work to do.

Gonzalo also had to attend to business so I decided to take myself off to Santiago's two daughters, Valparaiso and Viña del Mar, an hour away by car. Valparaiso is a sprawling town, known to sailors and corsairs from every corner of the globe as an essential port of call for any circumnavigator. As usual, British ships led the way: I visited a small cemetery especially for British sailors which was very moving as so many died young.

Valparaiso is built on steep hills and has been badly knocked about by earthquakes and tsunami waves, but it still retains historic charm. Near Chile's esteemed naval college on the waterfront, intending officers strutted crisply past. I admired one extremely well-designed building, a public library conceived and paid for by an erudite Briton who had done well out of maritime commerce. Its style was eighteenth century neoclassical with a flat roof and balustrade upon which stood statues of famous men since the time of Plato and Aristotle. There was Cervantes, Shakespeare and Newton but I was surprised to find Herbert Spencer, who extended Darwin's theory of improvement by natural selection to the human race. England was making fast progress with the Industrial Revolution and Spencer wrote books which he called the gospel of infinite improvement. Progress would make for ever better humans: Nature demanded it. His philosophy has been forgotten – after two world wars.

North-east of Valparaiso rises her younger sister, Viña del Mar, born as a seaside resort in the nineteenth century. There is a local textile and metal work industry, and the major source of income is tourism though dangerous tides often preclude bathing. On a hill overlooking the town is the Cerro Castillo palace, the summer home of Chile's president. I couldn't help being concerned by the large number of ten- and twelve-storey apartment blocks which looked like death traps in an earthquake.

Bernard was due back that evening and we had agreed Gonzalo should be our guest for dinner at our hotel. We chose a table with a view and our friendly waitress – an immigrant from ravaged Colombia – recommended the salmon from the mountain lakes. I tried a glass of their white Chardonnay and was impressed by the delicate bouquet of pineapple and lemon. It would go well with the fish.

Bernard told us about his ski-ing. There had been no hoists or lifts on the steep mountain slopes of the resort, but the sun shone from a cloudless sky and he enjoyed a long day's exertions. The one hotel near the slopes had been built and was still managed by Señor Tourville, a French entrepreneur. When he found out about Bernard's work as a microbiologist, he had offered him the night's lodging at half price.

Gonzalo knew the hotel because it regularly attracted skiers from the States. 'When you get back to France, tell your friends that we need more professional men like Tourville...'

Bernard described a church he'd chanced upon on his return. It claimed to possess the wooden crucifix Pedro de Valdivia carried with him all the way from Estremadura. 'I saw it above the high altar: very frail but still in good condition. So I bought a postcard and sent it to my daughters, to remind them to cram for their exams.'

'Slave driver!' I teased him.

'They are sixteen and seventeen: you have to keep a tight rein.'

'Do you think of earthquakes as warnings or punishment?' I asked him.

'I take it you're assuming a Judge.'

'Of course.'

'What, then, if the Judge is wholly good? And therefore merciful?'

Gonzalo bounced in. 'As I see it, earthquakes are built into Earth's foundations either by chance or purposely. They cause destruction and make rebuilding essential. In a country as poor as ours, we need that incentive. Otherwise we'd disappear altogether, just like Pompeii.'

'But how do you explain the killing of poor innocent victims?' insisted Bernard.

'Being good Catholics and innocent, they'll go straight to heaven.' I couldn't tell whether Gonzalo was being sarcastic or serious. But he was already talking about itineraries. 'Tomorrow early we fly to La Serena which boasts the clearest skies on Earth, then to Atacama, driest desert on Earth. After that, further surprises. It's only fair to warn you that Chile has long been known as the land God gave to Cain.'

CHAPTER SIX

Music and Poetry

La Serena – the serene one or the siren? In fact the word
means evening dew for this is a maritime town close to
burning desert where the clash of temperatures produces
plentiful and very welcome condensation.

A string of wide fine sand beaches glistened in the sun
keeping the high Pacific breakers at bay for as far as the eye can
see. This is the holiday resort for the region of El Chico Norte,
the Small North. It was first founded in 1544 on Valdivia's
orders to provide a sea link between Peru and Chile.

La Serena soon became the gateway for missionaries
following Valdivia's initiative in bringing Christ to a totally
pagan country. Religious orders from Spain, Italy and Germany
built hospices for the new arrivals and the city boasts twenty-
nine churches. In the absence of timber, some of these were
built from a sturdy species of bamboo. As a result, their high
central bell towers have survived severe earthquakes.

Gonzalo had arranged for us to lodge in the home of a
former fellow student and exile. Ken Ortega was tall and
muscular, with eyes that spoke of suffering. The ground floor
of his house had been opened out to make one large, well-lit
space serving as both living- and music-room. There were
cushioned settees at one end and an array of quaint musical

instruments at the other. The walls were hung with posters advertising troubadour groups, the largest inscribed La Paz y La Democracia. Gonzalo explained that Ken was one of the leaders of Chile's musical renaissance which began in the 1960s and soon turned into a full-scale social revolution.

On entering I was immediately struck by a drawing in sepia of an oval-faced young woman with a forceful chin and prominent lips. Her cheeks were pockmarked and her expression mournful. It was an unforgettable face worthy of Dürer. Ken explained that it was Violeta Parra, born into a poor family and moulded by a childhood bout of smallpox, who had pioneered this musical renaissance. In the early Sixties, she travelled the length of Chile collecting musical instruments played by tribes and minority groups.

He then showed us three such instruments, improvising on each. The *zampona*, an Andean flute similar to the panpipes, the *charango*, a small stringed instrument made from armadillo hide, played by strumming very fast, and the *bombo*, a huge booming Andean drum.

Violeta composed songs to be played by these instruments. The songs were often sad, reflecting her frustrated love life. But her most famous composition, *Gracias a la Vida*, is upbeat. Ken sang it to us first in Spanish, then in English as he played along on the guitar.

Gracias a la vida que me ha dado tanto,	Thanks to life which has given me so much,
Me dio dos luceros que cuando los abro,	It gave me two eyes and when I open them,
Perfecto distingo lo negro del blanco,	I can distinguish perfectly black from white,
Y en el alto cielo su fondo estrellado,	And in the infinite sky, its starry depths,

Y en la multitudes el hombre que yo amo.   And in the crowds, the man
                                              I love.

Under Violeta's leadership, this musical revolution emanating from the repressed minorities became a full-blooded political movement in favour of democracy and peace between poor and rich, between trade unions and iron-fisted government. Throughout the Sixties and Seventies, dozens of folk bands toured South America and Europe, winning support for the social revolution. In the United States, Joan Baez recorded Violeta's *Thanks to Life* in an album of the same name, a celebration of her own Spanish-American roots. Violeta herself toured widely with her songs, painting, sculpture and ceramics and her famous tapestries. Worn out by her exertions, with no money after yet another ill-fated love affair, Violeta wrote *Thanks to Life* shortly before killing herself in 1967.

Two of her children, Isobel and Angel, opened a music bar in Santiago which soon became the centre of the New Chilean Song Movement. Victor Jara, one of the foremost musicians of that era, a man of peasant stock but already established as a gifted theatre director and actor, performed folk songs and his own compositions at the bar. Soon he became the leading figure on the musical scene, a powerful political and educational voice for social change. Momentum for reform was to crystallize in the Popular Unity government led by Salvador Allende, a Communist doctor, who became President of Chile in 1970.

'My favourite song by Victor Jara is *The Plough*,' said Ken. 'This is the cry of the strongly-built peasant. Violeta's word was "sadness", Victor's is "self-confidence".'

He sang,

Aprieto firme mi mano   I grasp it tight in my hand
y hundo el arado en la tierra   And plunge the plough into the land

hace años que llevo en ella	All the years I have worked it.
¿cómo no estar agotado?	How could I not be worn out?
Vuelan mariposas, cantan grillos,	Butterflies fly, crickets sing,
la piel se me pone negra	My skin is burned black
y el sol brilla, brilla, brilla.	And the sun shines, it shines and shines.
El sudor me hace surcos,	The sweat runs off me in channels.
yo hago surcos a la tierra	I make channels in the earth without
sin parar.	end

Almost tearfully, Ken concluded, 'Three years after Allende became President, Victor Jara paid with his life for stating so powerfully the need for social change. Gonzalo knows better than I how that happened.'

Ken gave his version of the bitterly contested past. He recounted that, until 1970, there had been a clean fight between the haves and the have-nots which was symbolized by folk song as against classical music. After Allende became President, he had made two major mistakes which alarmed the Yankees: he was photographed with Fidel Castro handing him a machine gun, and he nationalized Chile's main source of income, the Chuquicamata copper mine, without paying any compensation. Despite Allende's efforts to help the poor, inflation soared and there were serious shortages due to strikes. The newly-appointed commander-in chief General Pinochet decided to make himself dictator: he brought in the army and bombed the presidential palace, whereupon Allende committed suicide. Opposition from Allende's followers was fierce and Pinochet responded by rounding up students and professors loyal to the Socialist party and sealing them in the National Stadium, where they were tortured and starved. Victor Jara was among them. A mocking guard ordered him to sing if he could, whereupon he recited *Vinceremos* – we will win – hymn of the Socialist party. His hands were broken and he was shot at until he died, the first of thousands tortured and killed on Pinochet's orders.

Ken's wife Teresa entered carrying a tray with glasses and a pitcher of Pisco Sour, the national drink. She explained that it was made from a pink muscatel variety of grape grown on the well-watered strip of land between La Serena and the desert. Three parts fermented grape juice were mixed with one part lemon juice, with the addition of sugar, one egg white and crushed ice. We sipped and declared it cool and uplifting. Somewhat at a loss for suitable words of appreciation, Bernard asked if it was a family recipe.

We asked whether Teresa was also a singer. 'I don't have a good voice but, before my marriage, I played violin in the National Symphony Orchestra. Now I take paying guests and act as part-time guide to show them our historic sites.'

Ken and Gonzalo had sunk into a deep gloom of reminiscence. 'Recent politics were more catastrophic than any earthquake,' Ken summed up grimly.

Bernard and I took this as our cue to go out for a stroll in the sun.

'Gonzalo isn't playing fair with me,' grumbled Bernard.

'In what way?'

'He knows very well I'm interested in the natural world. Instead, we get a hysterical replay of Communism versus Capitalism. Of Pinochet I'm sick to vomit.'

'I'm sure he doesn't mean to hurt your feelings. Remember, he was involved in that nightmare. He lost friends and family.'

Bernard shrugged and said he felt disappointed.

Before leaving England, I'd enjoyed dipping into the poetry of two great Chileans who both won the Nobel Prize for literature. The best known poem was Pablo Neruda's hymn to the natural richness of tropical Latin America, ruined by the conquistadors who cut down its forests and stole its wealth of gold. But what I really enjoyed were Gabriela Mistral's profoundly moving and highly personal lyrics. They were of a quality I'd rarely encountered save in the North American poets Frances Osgood and Emily Dickinson. Yet Mistral is little known in England.

I wanted to change the mood and asked about her. Gonzalo said she was born near La Serena and her house was now a small museum open to the public. A short drive took us from La Serena with its maritime climate up to the Valle de Elqui in the mountains, where the air was dry and the fertile land was planted with corn interspersed with clusters of fig trees. This was a more loveable Chile than the icy deep South.

Gonzalo sketched out Gabriela Mistral's unusual childhood. She was born in 1889 into a humble family and named Lucila Godoy de Alcayuga. Her childhood was spent in the Elqui valley under the watchful eye of her elder sister who was the local school- and post-mistress. Under the influence of her elder sister and her grandmother, who taught her the Bible, she decided aged fifteen to become a teacher in a nearby village. After taking her certificate, she taught in various places in Chile including Punta Arenas.

Using the pseudonym Gabriela Mistral, so named for the Archangel and the cold dry wind that blows across the Elqui valley, in 1914 she entered a national poetry competition and won the prize with *Los Sonetos de la Muerte*.

We arrived at the village of Montegrande and stopped outside the house where Gabriela spent her childhood. It was a plain unfurnished home with a few mementoes. Most notable was a bust of Gabriela's strong handsome head, her Amerindian blood showing in the high cheekbones, her Latin blood in the slim Roman nose and masculine chin.

'So powerful a face, yet such sensitive poems,' I murmured.

'She embodied all that is best in Chile: integrity, courage, patriotism,' Gonzalo responded.

When her poems won her fame in Latin America, Mistral travelled to Mexico at the request of the Minister of Education to assist in organizing that country's educational reforms. There she compiled *Lecturas para Mujeres*, a prose collection to help educate female readers, and she brought out her first book of poetry, *Desolación*, published in New York. Thereafter she travelled widely, first as a poet and lecturer, later as Chilean consul for twenty years. When awarded the Nobel Prize, she suggested that she won it because she was the candidate of women and children.

We walked up to a rocky outcrop overlooking the valley. 'She died aged sixty-eight in New York and was buried here, overlooking her childhood home.' Her gravestone was engraved with a quotation from her work: '*What the soul does for the body so does the poet for the people.*'

We returned to Ken's house and took our leave. 'Pack up now,' urged Gonzalo. 'We're leaving for La Silla Observatory. It's a two-hour drive: we're spending the night there as guests.'

We headed north, with Gonzalo driving and concentrating his attention on the winding road. Bernard was anxious we make a detour to see the fog harvesting project near the abandoned iron mine at El Tofo. A massive array of fine netting lay across the slopes to capture heavy coastal mist to provide water for local villagers. Gonzalo said the idea of harvesting water from fog came from observing droplets condensing on the leaves of eucalyptus trees. The project had been imitated in similar arid uplands elsewhere in South America and also in Oman.

Bernard was still feeling cross with Gonzalo. He was dubious about the merits of spending millions on observatories and high magnification telescopes. 'It's not that I'm against astronomy. One must learn what the Sun can give us. Years ago the French built a fantastically expensive complex disc which they promised would turn the Sun's rays into millions of volts of electric power. It never produced one unit of usable energy and stands rotting in the Pyrenees, a monument to man's hubris.'

'Are you saying that bold experiments are best avoided because they might turn out to be a waste of money?' asked Gonzalo incredulously.

'That's part of the reason. The main reason is that these experiments deceive us into thinking that man can know the mind of God.'

'Strong words, Bernard, but don't apply your reasoning to Chile,' said Gonzalo clenching his jaw in dismay.

We stared at the harsh landscape rolling past. 'This is desert in two senses,' observed Gonzalo after regaining his composure. 'There's no water and no settled population polluting the air with smoking fires. You see why this place is popularly known as Nearer Heaven!' He described how the surrounding hills were a favourite meeting place for esoteric cults and guru-led communities who interpreted the heavens quite differently from their neighbouring astronomers. 'Some believe in the power of the signs of the zodiac; others interpret shooting stars as heralds of a huge meteor that will crash into Earth and destroy all human life. One man swears he encountered an alien climbing out of his rocket, his face emitting bright light, who hurried to embrace the Earth man. But then he fell into a swoon for five hours and can't remember what happened next.' Gonzalo was giggling.

From miles off we spotted the white observatory casing like the dome of a mosque. As we drew nearer, we saw the aperture from which the famous telescope scanned the heavens, reminding me of an anti-aircraft gun. Next to it were single-storey buildings for the dozens of computers which translated the night's readings into statistics and complex language, as well as housing for staff and visitors.

Gonzalo left us to take a tour while he searched out the Director. Bernard was grumbling. 'I've spent twenty years using a magnifying glass to discover a cure for new forms of cancer. Why should I use it to look for water on Mars?'

'Because where there's water there may be life,' I replied.

'Bacilli at best,' he huffed.

'Remember Bernard, we're Gonzalo's guests.'

He pulled a face. 'Very well. But I'll treat it as a circus peep-show – free of charge.'

Darkness had fallen and a young member of staff offered to show us round. One telescope was occupied colour photographing a red dwarf, but its pilot telescope was free and I found myself peering at a small blur of weak light, its planet invisible.

I asked my guide to take me to a telescope where I could view violent collision within our galaxy.

'We can't offer you collision: distances between stars are too great for that. What we can show you is far more violent: the explosion of a giant star as seen by an artist.' He took me to a display of colour photographs of stars in our galaxy and the imagined stages in a supernova explosion.

'When a giant star explodes, it becomes a thousand million times brighter than the sun. That's when it's run out of nuclear fuel. It collapses because of its own gravitation, and runaway thermonuclear reactions follow. No one has witnessed a supernova explosion since the Chinese in AD 1054. Its tattered remains are clearly visible in the Crab Nebula.' He led us to a telescope pointed at the Taurus constellation. I saw a huge still bright patch of light, vastly greater than all the surrounding stars put together. 'These are the remains of the original super star,' explained our guide. 'Its outer layers have formed twisted filaments which give the nebula its name. The star's core collapsed and became a neutron star emitting radio pulses.'

Gonzalo came to fetch us over for our official welcome. We seated ourselves in a capacious office opposite a grey-haired man with friendly dark eyes and a strong chin. He turned to Gonzalo and said, 'I thank you my distinguished friend for finding the time to come with your European visitors. Ours is only one among many watchtowers scattered over five continents all scrutinizing the heavens for truth.'

After this modest preamble, he told us about his current interest. New studies based on observations of exploding stars – supernovae – appeared to show that the expansion of the Universe is accelerating. 'If praise is due, it should go to those who invented the instruments we use.'

The Director was excited by the possibility of there being planets like our own, but he was much exercised by the unrealistic claims made by some astrophysicists. He was upset by how only fantastic and tendentious speculations were seized upon by the world media.

Gonzalo was reassuring. 'But these speculations have their uses: they make the general public aware that the huge sums spent by today's astronomers are getting results they can understand. There is great appeal in the idea of other habitable worlds even if such planets are too distant to be visited by man.'

It was my turn to speak. 'What interests me is that, despite trying, we have never received any indication that there are other intelligent life forms out there. If there are humanoids on a distant planet, they would probably be entirely uninterested in receiving our signals, assuming they were still there by the time the signal arrived. But we have this basic human urge to find proof that we are not alone in the universe. We snatch at any lifeline, however flimsy. In my opinion, astronomers should be thinking less about invisible stars in remote galaxies and more about our unique planetary system. We need to try and harness the sun's fusion of hydrogen to generate immense power, and to correlate the Sun's changing magnetism with historic high and low temperatures to help us understand global warming.'

'Thank you for speaking so frankly,' said the Director. 'It is not for me to direct my staff's fields of research. But I will say that conversation at the dinner table often turns to the complex subject of global warming.'

'Don't you think astronomers should leave to cosmologists the current fashionable theory that the universe originated in a three-minute explosion and will eventually come to an end in a whimper? One man's pessimism has no more weight than another man's optimism.'

'Weisenberg's Big Bang theory is the source of much debate,' he acknowledged.

CHAPTER SEVEN

Valle de la Luna

A short flight from La Serena following the coastline brought us to Calama. In shape Chile resembles a giant thermometer in which the temperature rises steadily as you reach the top. We stepped into oven-hot air and peeled off our sweaters. Gonzalo donned a rancher's wide-brimmed leather hat, Bernard an immaculate white panama and I wore a fawn peaked cap picked up at a market stall in Valparaiso.

Sharp-eyed Bernard spotted the small stitching on my cap and read it aloud, "'*Club de los Grandes*". And who are the Great Ones – besides yourself of course?'

'Los Grandes indeed!' laughed Gonzalo. 'Whatever happened to English understatement?'

A dusty Landcruiser awaited us. We loaded our bags and, minutes later, we were heading east on a narrow traffic-free ruler-straight macadam road. Yesterday's plain had been modulated by rises and dips, but this one was totally level, flat as a dance floor, extending in every direction to the horizon, with no slope, bush or boulder to hold the eye. On and on we drove with no sense of advancing, for outside nothing changed.

'We seem to be getting nowhere,' I protested.

'Or perhaps this is Nowhere,' Bernard suggested drily.

'We call it the Plain of Patience,' Gonzalo said brightly.

'There's nothing to distract you from waiting.'

Another twenty minutes of threadbare patience with the heat building up aggressively. Gonzalo pulled off the road and we emerged into the intense glare, our feet treading dark grit.

Here, turning a full circle, we experienced the desert's amplitude, suggestive to me of an immense open prison then, more powerfully, a science fiction scene. Space had taken over. Swept clear of human clutter, earth was reduced to a flat disc, so empty as to be of no consequence in itself and merely serving as a departure and arrival area for interplanetary travel. I stared until my eyes began to smart, then picked up a palmful of the dryness and rubbed it between my fingers: shreds of moka-brown shale, parched and odourless, lifeless, incapable of life. Discarded leftover shavings from the work of creation.

In contrast, Bernard looked on admiringly. With his Latin blood, he appeared to welcome the heat. After scanning the emptiness, he lowered his binoculars, speechless. Wonder was not a state he chose to linger in and soon he was seeking out new information. Gonzalo was only too glad to oblige.

'Though we can't see them, two rows of mountains enclose this plain: the coastal *cordillera* we saw from the air and the High Andes. They build up and retain a high-pressure area impervious to moisture-bearing clouds. Hence this desert, earth's driest. Mercury can touch forty-one degrees: today it's a mild thirty-four.'

'And animal life?'

Gonzalo shook his head. 'Lichen.'

Bernard mimed an accusing air. 'You've set me down where there's no living thing to look at!'

We drove on for another twenty minutes and again Gonzalo pulled over. We were on a rise looking across a uniformly grey valley ruffled in low mounds and hillocks, some sharply crested and others smooth.

'Remember our speculations about melting glaciers? Here, in one warming period, melt water raised the sea level and floods swept over the Plain of Patience. This valley became a salt lake. In the course of centuries, all that water evaporated, leaving a deposit of salt gypsum. The wind has carved out these surrealist shapes. We call it the *Valle de la Luna*.'

I was dismayed by the bleak sterility all around.

'Look at it as one of Nature's jokes,' suggested Bernard gaily: 'made in the spirit of an eighteenth century Gothic folly.'

We crunched down a slope of greyish white particles, the colour of wood ash. Here and there, the mounds of gypsum assumed familiar forms: one was known locally as *Las Tres Marias*, but the cross beside them had crumbled.

Gonzalo took my arm. 'Not a stalk or leaf in sight. Nor will there be, with no water and virtually no rain. Before you conclude that it's useless, let me tell you that NASA flew in their prototype moon buggy, because this is the closest there is to lunar terrain.'

I said I missed the moon as it was before astronauts landed. 'Its light limned our night-time world. It inspired Shelley and Beethoven. But now we've photographed every pockmark on its face and it's been emptied of romance. Byron's lines have a new meaning, "We'll go no more a roving by the light of the moon."'

'This was scientific research,' objected Gonzalo. 'Surely we should welcome that.'

Bernard shook his head. 'Its immediate aim was political: to get there before Russia. And for the top level at NASA it was an act of hubris. Man decked himself out in giant's clothing to announce a giant step forward for mankind.'

As we drove on, coarse growth appeared out of the grey waste with more patches further on until we saw chlorophyll in the shape of weed on moist ground. Further still, we encountered patchy marsh bordered by reed and then a shallow pool. Here was fresh water flowing underground from the invisible Andes!

Thorn trees and curry-coloured adobe marked the first signs of human life in this remote oasis. The clay sediment was irrigated and planted with potatoes, maize and coca. Clay had been packed into rectilinear blocks to make neat firm walls; lintels for doors were hewn from thorn acacia, roofs thatched from reed. A dirt road led into the village and a dozen narrow lanes crossed it at right angles, each with its name painted on a wooden slat. The houses were single-storey, entered by a patched-up wooden door, with the top shutter ajar and serving as a window. The main alley led to a modest *plaza* with a central bandstand and, on the far side, two reassuring essentials: fire engine and church.

Atacameños have high cheekbones, dark tapering eyes and complexions which match the beaten earth they tread. I could believe this people had been fashioned like Adam out of local dust and so had a closer link than any other with the first moments of creation. Men went bareheaded and dressed in cotton vests and denims; women wore hats in a variety of styles, blouses with the occasional touch of colour and long ample skirts.

The inn where we were to spend the night was thatched, with clay-coloured walls in keeping with the rest. Each room had a glazed window looking onto a courtyard. Here the desideratum was shade, the deeper the better. Branches of a tall thorn acacia hung over a table and chairs; young ornamental plants in flower boxes enjoyed extra protection with a specially fitted overhanging trellis. We rested from the midday heat and slurped down bottled water.

Gonzalo read the political pages off the previous day's *Mercurio* while Bernard and I studied the map. Gonzalo had gone to a lot of trouble to bring us here and I had not responded to his lunar landscape. So I was pleased to be able to tell him that I warmed to this adobe village.

'It is unique,' he admitted. 'The challenge now is to keep it authentic.'

'That's a worldwide problem,' sighed Bernard. 'Take Lascaux and its Stone Age paintings. So many people want to see them that there's simply no space. They've run up a facsimile outside the cave and that's what visitors admire.'

'It's not just that we take up space, we also damage what we go to see, whether it's the humidity in our awe-struck breath or the tyre tracks we leave on your Valley of the Moon.'

Gonzalo nodded. 'Here's a unique village in a unique landscape. We have to beware the impact of package tourism on the people. If tourists flock in with totally opposed values, the Atacameños will start to feel less secure. They'll think they're backward and want to break with the past. The plight of Australian aborigines is there to warn us.'

We walked to the plaza which was noisy with chatter and children playing. The villagers had the quietly resolute look of those to whom nature has granted no favours. We stopped at a stall selling patterned woollens and carved artefacts. My eye was caught by a container the size of a coffee cup moulded from fawn-coloured fibres, an object for which it would be difficult to find a use. The trader explained that it had been made out of prickly pear and we laughed at this triumph of improbability. Ever mindful of microbes, Bernard warned us off buying an ice lolly off a cheerful woman wheeling a trolley.

'Let's turn the clock back four and a half centuries!' Gonzalo announced as we found some shade in which to step back in time. He conjured up the vision of Francisco Pizarro, who had fought his way into Inca Peru. His friend Pedro de Valdivia helped him save his leadership from rivals, then decided to explore southward on his own account. Pizarro gave him permission to take for himself and his followers any land he found. Gonzalo described Valdivia's appearance depicted in the portrait hanging in Santiago's town hall: Valdivia was strongly built and wore lightly his steel armour richly figured with beaten Inca gold. His long head and full jaw carried an air of authority underlined by the black pointed moustache and tufted beard. This was the man who rode south with a dozen followers and his faithful mistress, Inés de Suárez. Entering Chile's temperate zone, he liked what he saw and, after fighting off attacks from the fiercest of the tribes, the Mapuche, he founded Santiago on the Mapocho Valley, naming it after Spain's patron saint. While he and his men were away, Mapuche warriors returned to attack the new settlement and were famously fought off with Inés de Suárez in chain mail leading the defence.

Valdivia also faced threats from his fellow-Spaniards. Conquistadors settled in Bolivia were demanding an outlet to the sea and were poised to over-run Chile's northern territories. In order to defend his possessions, Valdivia marched north to look for a possible garrison post near the mountain passes from which his enemy was likely to attack. Suddenly this desert oasis faced visitors swathed in metal armour and carrying swords. The new arrivals decided that the place was suitable as a defence post and so they stayed, renaming it San Pedro de Atacama.

The small archaeological museum gave an insight into Atacameño culture. These were farmers who grazed llamas, wove cloth and baskets. We surveyed the tools made of bone, wood and stone: spoons, pestles, baskets of cactus fibre, bone needles. There was little sign of development.

Balanced atop wooden tables with knees drawn up tightly against their cheeks were hundreds of well-preserved mummies which had been found in ancient graves together with mastodon bones. Gonzalo explained how mummification was

71

a consequence of the dry climate. 'Bury a body here and it will not decompose. So you remove the intestines and let the body dry out slowly. The mummy provides a capsule for the spirit of the dead one. Like rose petals in a pot-pourri.'

Bernard drew our attention to some child mummies with cranial deformations. Flat boards were attached to the top of the skull using woollen yarn. 'Perhaps it was an attempt to correct some imperfection,' he suggested.

'Strange to leave the boards in place, as if they remain part of the child's identity, as if they were meant as ballast for a still not fully formed spirit that might otherwise be dispersed,' I ventured.

The curator, a local man, maintained that the boards served to flatten and enlarge the forehead and that this was a mark of social distinction.

Gonzalo started laughing. 'See how quickly we part company, each clinging to his own guess. Until we know the origins of an event, we can't begin to understand it.'

'But we enjoy the speculation,' I said. Burial customs usually reflected attitudes to an afterlife, I suggested. The Romans believed only in hell and so cremated their dead. Jewish Pharisees expected a pleasant afterlife and buried their dead in expensive tombs wrapped in sweet-smelling spices. The early Christians buried in catacombs and later in graveyards in expectation of heaven. Muslims also clung to burial. 'But with space so short in cities, and society overwhelmingly secular, we've gone back to the Roman practice of cremation.'

'Burning takes less time, and time is money,' said Bernard bleakly.

The church of San Pedro was an imposing building: an archway set off a plain rectangular structure with whitewashed walls and pitched roof. Next to it rose a squat belfry surmounted by a cross. Inside, the light flooded in from the open doorway; heavy beams hauled up from the coast by mule made possible a high ceiling conducive to worship. A plain altar and tabernacle stood against the east wall flanked by plaster statues of favourite saints rigged out in the colourful finery appropriate to paradise. But numbers had fallen and, whereas there had once been a resident priest, now a priest from Calama came on alternate Sundays.

To assist our imaginative journey into the past, Gonzalo had hired horses, no beauties but strong and willing. We trotted in terrain as flat and desolate as the Plain of Patience but coloured in every shade of grey, with Gonzalo cheerfully likening us to the handful of roughnecks who accompanied Pedro de Valdivia from Peru.

'Valdivia was an incorrigible optimist. "There is soil to sow," he wrote to Pizarro, "materials for building and water and grass for animals; it seems as if God had created everything so that it would be at hand." He didn't say a word about Chile's ninety per cent wastelands: that would have deterred future venturers.'

With patriotic verve, Gonzalo told us that Chile's conquistadors showed more respect for the native inhabitants than Spaniards elsewhere in Latin America. But I had read somewhere that the Mapuche possessed sizeable amounts of local silver and gold and that Valdivia made forays to seize their wealth by force.

I asked Gonzalo if it was true that the Mapuche had captured Valdivia on Christmas Day and put him to death by forcing him to swallow molten gold.

Gonzalo replied coldly, 'There are different accounts of his death, all gory and all apocryphal since none of Valdivia's party survived the battle.'

An hour's brisk trot on a bumpy track brought us to a wooden pavilion where a full-time guard was posted to protect the national heritage site and to warn off trekkers. We tethered our horses and started walking towards the salt lake. We came first to an immense expanse of grey-white filigree orbs such as might decorate a Christmas tree. Thousands of them blobbed out of the ground, but they were barbed and knife-sharp to the touch. Gonzalo explained that the whole expanse consisted of lumps of salt eroded and wrinkled by the wind. 'If you value your shoes, don't walk on them,' he warned and guided us along a narrow track of banked-up earth that led to the lake edge.

On even the calmest sea there will be a play of light suggestive of life within the deep; in this expanse of matt white extending to the horizon I could detect no glint, no extra dimension, nothing mysterious. For all its immensity, I could see it only as a dead end, a double-blank domino.

Gonzalo was enraptured by the geology. 'We're looking at the remnants of an immense inland sea. The scorching sun blow-dried it to create a salt mausoleum as opposed to the other Moon landscape which was made of gypsum.'

At the edge of the salt flat a pair of flamingoes were swinging their long necks, dredging up minute organisms from the puddle-shallow water. The sight conjured up a vision of swinging croquet mallets until Bernard brought me back to reality as he explained how the Andean flamingo differed from its various cousins. The plumage was a pale pink, with bright upper feathers and a patch of black on the wing; the legs were yellow to match the large yellow and black bill.

'How many pairs are there?' he asked.

'Just 20 or so,' said Gonzalo. 'Mainly here, where the salt bed is thin and patchy.'

'I suppose they nest on mud mounds with no cover. Any predator with long-range vision can just swoop down on the fledglings.'

'Exactly. It's the sport of the condor, our national bird.'

Bernard summed up the situation with a smile. 'Micro-organisms rise from a salt flat in just two stages to fuel the lord of your skies.'

The three of us gazed at the white expanse. 'Out there, it's not just landmarks that disappear, but also sounds,' said Gonzalo. 'The salt flat is silence made visible and that can be frightening. At first, you resist by humming or singing or reciting poetry, only to find you're reduced still further to something very ridiculous. Some days a heat haze blurs the horizon and you could swear that you see distant houses, trees, people and animals on the move, even pools of water.'

'It puzzles me,' said Bernard by way of answer. 'It's so vast and looms up like a giant question mark. Life in a living cell is what I know – carbon and water, mostly water. In the human body, cells work with amazing economy. There is nothing superfluous, no waste, everything fits. But here we have just the opposite: huge wastes, over-abundance of shale, gypsum, salt, and no water. The purposeful microscopic world that I cling to is dwarfed in this geology.'

Gonzalo's gaze was lost in the distance. 'This *salar* extends over a hundred kilometres. It's never been properly mapped, probably can't be. Boundaries shift, tracks disappear as soon as they're made. Just recently, two amateur geologists set off to cross it. Halfway into their trip, their vehicle hit a rock and the axle was smashed. In just two days hypothermia sucked them bone dry.'

'One more dead end region,' I mused. I believed earth was made for man, yet here was an utterly inhospitable place. I shared my thoughts with Bernard. 'Remember how Daniel calls on all the inanimate works of the Lord to give Him praise? Clouds of the sky, sun and moon and stars, showers and rain, breezes and winds, cold and heat, dew, frosts and snow, fountains and springs, mountains and hills, rivers and seas. The

Psalmist too. Almost everything gets invoked, but not the desert of Judea nor the Dead Sea, which would have been known to them. Is it possible that they didn't see desert and salt lake as works of the Lord? Because that's what I feel about this salt flat.'

'The Dead Sea is alkaline, not salt. But I take your point. Look at it this way: the desert was where Christ was three times tempted to prove his divinity with a miracle, and He resisted. Perhaps desert or salt flat or any lifeless hostile terrain is where we feel confused, lost and where we too are tempted…'

'Tempted to experience Satan?'

'More provoked into doubt by Satan.'

'Doubt about Christ's power?'

'Doubt about the very existence of God.'

Gonzalo shook us out of our reverie. 'Tomorrow we'll look for more animals to satisfy Bernard,' he chuckled. 'But we'll need to do some stiff climbing.'

We returned to the car and headed for our inn and rest.

CHAPTER EIGHT

Springs of Life

Next day called for an early start as we wanted to reach the geysers of Tatio before sunrise. At four o'clock, half-asleep, I piled on sweaters for the mountains ahead and climbed into a waiting Land Rover. Unwilling to negotiate a precipitous road in the darkness, Gonzalo had engaged a driver from San Pedro.

We drove northward. Our track ran up and down steep slopes. Dozing despite the lurching motion of the jeep, we woke two hours later to see another stretch of perfectly flat terrain devoid of vegetation. Dawn's first light was checked by a low band of mist, vapour rising from the ground.

Stepping out, we saw the vapour originated in water-sogged earth here in the driest of deserts. We registered astonishment, much to Gonzalo's satisfaction. 'These are springs of fresh water, warm rising to very hot, bubbling up to welcome you in a hundred different shapes. Take a closer look while I cook breakfast.'

On every side, water spurted into the air, cocking a snook at gravity. Bernard crouched beside one pool after another, searching for unusual beetles or water-bugs, only to rise empty-handed but still persistent while I pressed on into a pathless maze of fountains, some gurgling timidly, others bubbling noisily and leaping high into the air. So much water evoked childhood memories of shady ponds where sprites and sylphs were said to sport. Water brought thoughts of beginnings, freshness, innocence, and mist, like scent, can impart mood.

We rejoined Gonzalo, bent over a steaming pool, busy retrieving newly hard-boiled eggs. He was impatient to resume the geology lesson. As we broke the shells off our eggs, he explained how the iron and other heavy elements lying deep in the earth's inmost core come under intense pressure from six thousand kilometres of rock pushing down from above. These elements ignite and explode, forcing molten rock to well up towards the earth's surface where it meets groundwater. As the geyser fills, the water at the top of the column cools off but, because of the narrowness of the vent, convective cooling of the water in the reservoir is impossible. The cooler water above presses down on the hotter water below until the water in the reservoir becomes superheated and is forced out in jetting pulses.

This network of geysers and hot springs was warmed by the magma which had surged up to form the nearby chain of high peaks topped by the Tatio volcano, shaped like a flattish cone and presently inactive. Chile's volcanoes were the result of the convergence between tectonic plates squeezing molten rock upward through denser surrounding rock. As it reached the crust, the magma spread out, forcing aside unheated rock, to gather in underground chambers up to six Olympic stadiums in size. Further pressure from below caused the magma to spurt up through a pipe-like conduit from which it fountained out as lava.

'So a volcano acts as a safety valve for excessive heat?' I asked.

'Yes, and in releasing pressure, it brings new rock to the surface. Chile has two thousand volcanoes, fifty of them still active. They make up a large number of the Andes peaks.'

Bernard showed interest. 'Would you say that much of the world we live in was created by volcanoes?'

'Exactly.'

'But if the earth's centre lies six thousand kilometres from the surface and our deepest borehole goes no deeper than twelve kilometres, then your hypothesis of a molten iron core forcing intense heat upwards cannot be tested scientifically.'

'It's the likeliest explanation for Earth's magnetic field. Measured temperature to twelve kilometres' depth can be extrapolated for increasing depths down to the core. As for heated fluid expanding and rising to displace cooler material, that's a ground rule of physics.'

'The Greeks and Romans saw it more simply,' I said. 'For them, the volcano was the one-eyed giant Cyclops. He usually slept but, when he awoke, his single eye burst open and then he was always bad-tempered and violent, apt to hurl flaming projectiles and let off toxic vapours.'

The sun was rising and we could now see the contours of the Tatio volcano. Gonzalo cheerfully suggested a hot dip. One of the geysers spouted near a natural hollow, the size of a dog-splash bathing pool filled with clear inviting water. Bernard and I waded in, while Gonzalo stripped off at a little distance and ran to join us. Bernard favoured an elegant backstroke, Gonzalo underwater sorties, while I chose to float and watch the steam rising. After colliding several times, we took to seeing who could duck the others most effectively.

Gonzalo was first to heave himself out and raced to where he had left his clothes, while Bernard and I slowly dressed by the pool.

'Did you notice those red lines on Gonzalo's legs?' I asked. 'My father had similar scars after surgery to extract clogged arteries.'

'Gonzalo's are different. I fancy they're from wounds designed to extract information.' Bernard hugged himself against the cold.

'By torture, you mean?'

'At the time of the Algerian war, one Paris hospital had a ward just for electrode burn cases.'

'He never let on to me.'

'Nor me.'

'Perhaps he wanted to forget.'

'Or perhaps he wants us to forget Pinochet's horrors. It offends his patriotism.'

Gonzalo rejoined us and, as we dried off, we realised the fountain display had slackened. It was as though the taps had been turned half off: the highest jets were now only chest high, their proud displays faltering. Gonzalo explained that, as the sun rose, the air was warmed and convection reduced. 'An hour from now, the springs will have disappeared – until dawn tomorrow.' He gave us a conspiratorial smile, like a conjuror's after a sleight of hand.

Bernard noticed an isolated lump of metal, the size of a heavy wardrobe. It might have been another of those abstract iron constructs favoured by Hispanic taste, a salute not to wind but to thermal water. Closer inspection showed it to hold a network of rusting pipes, the relic of a larger unit for generating electricity from boiling water.

Gonzalo shrugged off any suggestion of failure. 'A brave experiment. It taught us a lot. One day we'll have geysers generating electricity, as they do in Japan.'

Considering we were three hours from the nearest village, Gonzalo's claim rang outlandish. I saw the discarded hulk as a sad monument to man's futility when pitted against hostile terrain. I might have voiced my sentiments except that seeing Gonzalo's scars had made me feel protective. Gonzalo had offered us this journey, this chance to see his country, a country for which he had suffered exile and worse. I did not want to disappoint him.

We retraced our route to rejoin the mountains. As we climbed, we turned onto a rough track which twisted between boulders across a shoulder of the first foothill. Rocks pitched us sideways as we jolted up the steep slope with no sight of bird or animal life.

At one point our engine stalled and the starter's repeated efforts failed to stir it. Anyone stranded here would be lost: there was no reliable contoured map, no water, no berries, not even a cave for shelter. Nature had shut and locked her door against any form of life.

As the gradient stiffened, we fastened our seat belts though the Land Rover had now slowed to walking pace. Gonzalo scanned the ground with field glasses and occasionally motioned a change of direction with a flick of his hand.

Rising expectancy was dwindling to frustration when, at a curt word from Gonzalo, the driver braked. From my window, I could see at a shotgun's range a flurry of scampering greyish brown creatures, like squirrels but larger, with tufted rabbity ears.

We followed Gonzalo. He was searching for a nook from which to spy without being seen. Then he beckoned us up to a dip behind a ledge of broken rocks where the spaces between provided peepholes. We wriggled down until our eyes were level with a gap and we could see ahead. On a platform of rock a cricket pitch distant, a group of *viscacha* sat motionless as though sunning themselves, while others darted between the rocks.

In our wide swathe of Atacama, these were the only wild creatures we had encountered apart from the flamingoes. Doubtless other animals lay concealed, but these for us were pristine: set against the desolation and stillness of the mountain, they seemed like a new creation. Their smallness made them appear pathetically vulnerable yet as a community they were assured enough to disport themselves in the open.

Gradually we picked out detail. Some were twice the size of others and wore a white smudge extending to the cheeks above a black mouth and long black drooping whiskers. The large heads looked cartoonish and mischievous and I was eager to get a closer look.

A swaggering male appeared on the platform to parade before the group. Slowly he edged towards the incumbent male. As though prompted by a puppet master, the rivals started to beat their tails, stamp their feet and emit a crescendo of squeals, grunts, moans and deep cries.

'They've spotted us,' I murmured.

'No. It's just a quarrel. Helps to liven a dull day.'

We carried on spying, finding it droll to see how the duo played out provocative tilts and exaggerated signs of fear: the performance was worthy of trained mimes.

Our driver had taken advantage of the uproar to crawl close to the platform. He had with him a round net edged with small lead weights which, after carefully taking aim, he tossed over the closest male. As the rest of the tiny troupe fled to nearby burrows, Gonzalo ran up to untangle the captive. Holding the head tight to prevent it biting, he rocked the viscacha back and forth, while describing its habits and scant diet of dry roots and lichens. 'Gnawing distinguishes this little creature, *Lagidium viscacia*, from his lowland cousin in Argentina,' said Gonzalo as Bernard's gloved hands investigated its wire-stiff whiskers, soft ears and razor-sharp incisors.

What struck me first was that the little scamperer sported a white moustache. Though different in colour and size from Bernard's, I couldn't help wondering whether the moustache might have a long pre-human history as a mark of masculinity.

Knowing Bernard regularly handled rats and mice for experimentation, Gonzalo passed him the animal. Bernard stroked away its fear and made soothing noises. He plumped the thick pads on its soles which enabled it to climb steep rocks. Turning it over, he examined its rump. 'Bone penis. No fiddling around. Is he prolific?'

'Seven litters of two over a ten-year life span.' Gonzalo estimated its weight at seven or eight kilos, double that of the female. He said the female was also moustachioed and my idle speculation was knocked for six. The firm bushy tail provided balance but was dispensable, he explained. If caught by a predator, the viscacha could still escape for the tail tore easily from its attachment, much as a cheque tears from its perforated stub.

Gonzalo explained that the viscacha's incisor teeth grew about a third of an inch a week. At lower altitudes, the excess growth would be worn away naturally in the process of eating nuts, hard seeds and tough vegetable matter. 'Up here the food is unabrasive. If left unchecked, the incisors would grow to the point where they clamped the jaw shut.' At some stage, three new muscles took shape which allowed the jaw to rotate back and forth as well as sideways. By holding a stone between the incisors and the lower jaw, the viscacha could check excessive growth, wearing away the soft dentine at the front and leaving the hard enamel on the back to form a chisel edge.

'Let's give this *chiquitito* his freedom and have a look at where he lives.' Our captive raced away beyond the platform and out of sight. We followed and came on a warren of burrows from which Gonzalo reckoned there were some forty viscachas in the community.

He then drew our attention to a different lot of hideouts made up of narrower earth burrows. These he said belonged to a different member of the same species, the chinchilla, a close relative. The creature slept in the burrow from dawn till dusk. Smaller and lighter, with just a short tail, the chinchilla emerged at night: hence his highly-prized fur, to keep him well wrapped-up. Forty or so hairs emerge from a single follicle to provide the warmth he needs. The chinchilla also has very large eyes capable of seeing in the dark and an enlarged bony cover of the middle ear to detect nocturnal predators.

Gonzalo paused to let Bernard state the implied puzzle.

'How is it that nature, mutation, instinct or whatever chose two such different paths in order to adapt to the same altitude and terrain and provide in each case the necessary structures?'

'And the puzzle deepens if we add that a third descendant of the assumed common ancestor – hamster or similar – is a lowland creature which protects its small body not with fur but with needle-sharp quills. The porcupine!'

I was beginning to discern Gonzalo's view of evolution: living organisms are programmed to be dynamic, exploratory, inventive – and as unpredictable as volcanic eruptions.

The rodents led my own thoughts in a different but reassuring direction. Earth's huge expanses of repellent waste might be dangerous to man but nonetheless offered a few brave little creatures the means to life. I could imagine that, on Day Six of his creative work, God had had the viscacha and chinchilla in mind, not just Adam and his descendants.

Bernard's mood had become brighter, almost cheerful, and improved still further when the driver ran to us saying he'd glimpsed a male puma. At once, the three of us, crouching low, started edging our way from cover to cover, up the steep slope to the vantage point he indicated.

The puma is a jaguar that's exchanged yellow and black pyjamas for a light brown coat providing almost perfect camouflage. The slow gliding gait raises no dust and it was some time before we spotted it, advancing cunningly between boulders and outcrops to within twenty metres of the playing viscachas. Stealthily it narrowed the gap until one viscacha, perched on a prominent rock to warm itself, uttered a sharp cry. This set the whole group scurrying into their burrows. With a growl of annoyance, the puma loped away and we slithered back to our vehicle.

Bernard proposed that to Gonzalo's two basic factors in evolution – terrain and climate – a third should be added: self-defence. This they discussed as we headed back to San Pedro.

CHAPTER NINE

Copper that Lights the World

B ernard kept his satellite phone in his overnight bag in case the hospital had to send any urgent messages. On the eve of our departure, he received news which left him anxious. I asked him if he was worried about one of his child patients.

'I'm worried, but not about a patient.' He turned to Gonzalo and asked if there would be Mass next morning at Calama.

Gonzalo nodded. 'Usually at ten. But travellers are dispensed.'

'I must get to that Mass.' Quiet but firm.

Gonzalo frowned. 'Our private tour of Chuquicamata mine is for 9.30.'

'I'll join you there after Mass.'

'You won't be allowed in. We'll have to take the public tour at eleven.'

We left for Calama at sunrise. From steep hairpin dirt tracks, we turned back onto the Road of Patience, leaving the brave community in Atacama to its solitary struggle against salt desert, black sandstorms and drought. Concerned at their lack of medical facilities, Bernard confided that he felt like a deserter. My reaction was more selfish. Instead of the amazement I'd experienced on the outward journey, the dark brown desert like an overcooked pancake seemed to sum up the dark and insidious aspects of all we had encountered since Puerto Natales.

On arrival, Bernard left us to walk to a nearby church and Gonzalo asked if I knew the reason for his sudden piety.

'Perhaps an infected mouse has escaped from his lab,' I suggested flippantly.

'I believe it may be more personal. You know his treatment involves injecting stem cells from a mother's placenta to replace lost bone marrow. According to reports I've been reading, Americans are finding stem-cells from embryos more effective than placenta cells... Bernard's research is State-funded.'

'So if he's being told to switch to the American method... Would the French do that?'

'Why not?'

Suppose Gonzalo's reading was near the mark? Bernard the leading leukaemia specialist would confront Bernard the convinced Catholic: surely a profound and troubling dilemma. I thought back to Bernard's way with the viscacha. His manner was neither one of clinical detachment nor of idle curiosity: it was something more like sheer pleasure at fondling life under a new form.

We walked to the mine office to cancel the private tour. After identifying himself, Gonzalo was handed a short email message. One of Santiago's State lawyers had tracked him down. Gonzalo read the message and looked shaken. He put a hand to his brow and closed his eyes. I could see what was written. 'Will you agree to testify?' read the message. A moment later he snapped, 'Be good enough to answer Yes. Nothing more.'

Walking back, I hoped he would confide in me but, no, I was left to speculate. Against whom was he going to testify? I knew that many Chileans wanted Pinochet prosecuted for having ordered the disappearance of some 2,000 men and women. Though influential, surely Gonzalo would not be involved in so tendentious a law suit. Then I recalled the scars on his muscular legs. Perhaps he was being asked to give evidence against one or more of his torturers. It was too sore a subject for me to inquire; I let it go.

Chuquicamata mine is a ten-minute drive from Calama. A broad road on rising ground narrows to streets of labourers' housing interspersed with numerous two-storey administrative buildings. Alongside run fenced areas holding machinery, some new, some decrepit having served their time in a complex that has been functioning for eighty years. No trees, no hint of colour; every surface dusted grey.

Outside the visitors' building we waited until a brisk lady arrived with the key. Tickets were issued and we were all led to benches and asked to remove our shoes. I caught Bernard's eye. 'After church, the mosque?'

We walked on stockinged feet to a wicket where a pair of hands exchanged our footwear for stout workmen's shoes with thick soles. Once these were laced up, we took our seats in the company bus and were driven up, down and up again to an open space atop one of the mine's massive tailings. Here we crossed on foot to a purpose-built belvedere. This was no ordinary belvedere, for it offered no pretty vista. Before us gaped a monstrous chasm. As a whale is to a herring, so this was to a typical gravel quarry. Rock enough to build a town had been wrenched from Mother Earth, not just skimmed off but gouged out deep enough to shelter a fifteen-floor building. The sides had been shaped to allow a succession of shelves around the perimeter, just wide enough to take heavy lorries, the whole suggestive of tiered seating in an amphitheatre. It was almost as though Rome's Colosseum, enlarged perhaps ten times, had been rammed deep into the earth.

On the perimeter shelves, towering crane scoops attacked the mine face, loosening rock blasted daily at dawn by dynamite and heaving it into huge wheeled trucks. Their operators too distant for us to see, one could suppose a malignant new species of insect had devised machinery for disembowelling our planet on the lines of those ants in my favourite schoolboy serial that gnawed away the iron supports of Scotland's Forth Bridge.

Gonzalo was watching my stupefied face. 'Close your eyes and picture the place ninety years ago. Just one more stretch of arid waste land. Good for nothing, you'd say. Godforsaken. But hidden deep within lies hidden treasure.' He laughed at my embarrassment and I joined him. Hadn't he said Chile would offer surprises?

The tour guide sketched the genesis of metallic ore. When Planet Earth began to form, cosmic dust cohered to its spinning sphere, with heavier particles such as metals being drawn towards the core. In time, pressure from above and intense heat resulted in explosions which carried metals up into earth's mantle. Pressure on specific areas caused new explosions that shattered the surrounding rocks into millions of fragments. Boiling water flooded in to penetrate the pieces. The resulting solution of copper sulphide seeped through the networks of tiny fractures and recemented them. The end result: many millions of tons of accessible copper ore.

Thirty-tonne trucks heaved ore from the pit face to ground level. A specimen wheel off one of these trucks was on display: twice a man's height in diameter with a huge balloon tyre that needed replacing every four months. To prevent the tyres from igniting, each truck was preceded by a motorized cistern to water the burning-hot track.

Vast quantities of water were needed to separate copper-bearing mineral from useless rock. The River San Salvador, riding high in the Andes, happened to flow just five kilometres from Chuquicamata: its course was diverted.

We were issued with thick protective jackets, metal helmets and gas masks and entered a high-roofed hangar bustling with workmen and ear-splitting as a battlefield. Giant iron cauldrons suspended by chains were being shunted about, clangorous as a trash metal rock band while beneath, on a steel platform linked to the floor by catwalks and fed with partially refined copper by ladder hoists, a giant gas fire blazed at around 1,000° centigrade.

The lower section of the furnace swung slowly open and out came a cauldron on pivots. It came to a stop above a cast-iron cradle suspended from the roof. Slowly the cauldron tilted until, from its lips, there issued a flow of molten metal, white-hot and syrupy.

The cauldron emptied, workmen swung the cradle to ground level where the metal would be left to cool with impurities being released as gas through blister-like holes. Then the copper would be moulded into rectangular plates two centimetres thick, the size of a tabloid newspaper.

We walked from the heat and din of the foundry to a hangar holding large rectangular pools of liquid. The air was cool and activity was limited to an occasional workman lifting frames from one of the pools.

Masks were no longer obligatory and Bernard eased his off. Unfolding a white handkerchief and with an expression of distaste, he wiped the perspiration from his forehead and the corners of his eyes. He turned grumpily to Gonzalo. 'The heat in there was stifling. Haven't they heard of air ducts?'

Gonzalo shrugged. 'Try smelting copper in an air-conditioned lab!'

'Some of those catwalks sag like rope bridges… As for those clouds of dust from the mine face!'

Gonzalo took the criticism calmly. 'Employees get regular check-ups and incipient silicosis cases are laid off for six months.'

'What of those chimneys spouting effluvia?'

Gonzalo returned a pat answer. 'Eight-five per cent of damaging particles have been eliminated and, five years hence, all emissions will be harmless. But arsenic contamination of groundwater remains a challenge.'

He motioned us to the pools of liquid. Here the last stage of refining occurred. Copper plates were hung on frames, thousands in each pond, suspended in a blue solution of water and sulphuric acid through which an electric current was passed. After two weeks' immersion, the plates were removed and dried. Gonzalo tapped on a loaded trolley as it was being wheeled away.

'When they started mining here, the ore yielded thirty-five per cent copper. Now it's down to just three per cent.'

'And if it falls further?'

Gonzalo shrugged. 'We must find new deposits. That's my department. We have three teams currently prospecting...'

'So all will be well?'

He met my eyes. 'The Altiplano is an area of great beauty, it's protected national parkland ... Nothing in Chile is simple.'

Gonzalo picked a plate off a trolley. It gleamed like a newly minted sovereign, like a dish from Tutankhamen's tomb. It seemed scarcely credible that, only a month before, its constituents had been lying unseen two hundred metres down a crater. What had awed us earlier in the day was molten and here it lay tamed, docile, tractable for man to make use of as he wished.

Gonzalo explained that the plate was now 99.9 per cent pure, the best obtainable and much prized. It would be shipped abroad, mainly to Korea and Japan. Its purity made it an ideal clearway for electric current so it would be processed into wire, thousands of kilometres of wire, much of it laid underground. Earth back to earth, but not to rest. Day in, day out, the thread-thin paths of light would keep darkness at bay in the scattered homes of Asia.

We set off back to Calama where the shops were all busy but the few restaurants were not yet open save one. Here the burly owner got up from helping his son repair a bicycle tyre to take us to a table. He handed us a menu with a flourish: it offered a set lunch of rump steak, T-bone steak or fillet steak. Clearly he catered for miners.

Over coffee Gonzalo drew my attention to a brawny man and his wife in Sunday best who had taken a nearby table. He wanted me to note how healthy their two small sons looked. 'We look after their children's health and education. It's the best we can do. Those hundreds of miners, truck drivers, smelters are doing a risky job that would kill you and me. Forget footballers: these are Chile's real heroes. And granted, the mine is a great scar on the landscape, but the rock, the fire in the smelters, the water, the cranes and drills and trucks are all gifts from Mother Earth. She looks silent, impoverished and grim but she has a heart of gold in the shape of marketable copper.'

Bernard sipped slowly from his cup looking abstracted. Gonzalo probed his reaction.

'It's not so much the health conditions that bother me: it's Chuqui as an undertaking. I'm from Paris where life is squeezed between blocks of apartments and offices, streets of noisy traffic, crowded shops. For city-dwellers like me, Earth isn't even a backdrop: it's off-stage. Since it doesn't lend itself to amusing remarks, I ignore it. But some of my friends are on earthquake call. They fly out to Turkey, Iran or whatever to dig survivors out of shattered buildings and sew them up. I realize that Earth is a box full of dirty tricks called floods, tidal waves, earthquakes and eruptions. It leads me to conclude that Earth is no friend to man and I go back to ignoring it. But I am struck now by the idea of copper creating paths of light. Thanks to those paths of light, a whole universe of proteins and DNA, stem cells and cancerous tissue which lay hidden from Day One, is made visible. Without those paths of light, no electron microscope, no X-rays, no gene analyser. I am thinking of the current transmitted along those paths. Generated in power stations built with steel and fuelled by oil and gas drilled from deep within the earth. Everything achieved by biological research is dependent on what Earth has placed within our reach. What I am saying is this, Gonzalo: you've presented me with something I find very stimulating, a paradox.'

I brooded on his words and recalled his earlier anxiety. If the chain of human life had been built up through millions of years, was he troubled by the idea of breaking it in his research lab?

We walked out into the hot bright sunshine. The plane to our next destination, Arica, Chile's northernmost city, left early that evening so we had a few hours to kill. We went to the one hotel that catered to an international clientele, mainly connected to the business of the copper mine, where we rested.

When we regrouped, Gonzalo was not his usual buoyant self. He told us that he'd received a threatening message on his mobile. 'Instruct your lawyer to halt legal proceedings – or else.'

'Who would issue such a threat?' I asked.

Gonzalo couldn't be sure. 'I haven't even started legal proceedings... Let's forget it and order a bottle of Chile's best Cabernet.'

He poured a little into Bernard's glass and invited him to pronounce it corked or too old. Bernard savoured the bouquet, nodded assent, then tasted the contents, leaving some on his palate. 'Not bad for a wine that isn't French,' he conceded.

Gonzalo smiled. 'The French vine used to make this wine was planted years before epidemic destroyed every one of France's vines.'

93

CHAPTER TEN

A Dangerous Town

It was dark when we landed at Arica's coastal airport. A pre-arranged car speeded us round an extensive estuary which twinkled with reflected lights. As we came to the first houses, we passed beneath a large banner courtesy of Pepsi Cola which welcomed us with the motto ARICA FOREVER. Further ahead, whitewashed stones proclaimed the same fatuous message. I took these to be signs of insecurity for Arica was Peruvian until 1883 when Chile annexed the town: Peruvian officers still swear an oath to repossess Arica. Now a container port and manufacturing base for anchovy fish meal, Arica has a reputation for being raw and tough.

We slept in a hotel north of the town and woke to find ourselves in parkland. We had breakfast alfresco, close to an enclosure holding two llamas, with the scent of oleanders mingling oddly with whiffs from the distant fish meal plant.

Our time in Arica was short and we headed straight for the major landmark. El Morro is a high rock headland with an almost flat summit the size of two playing fields. It had withstood the sea's erosive force to become a defensible bastion: around its rim were ranged the canons that had decimated Peruvian assailants.

Gonzalo had brought us for a seagull's view of the port below and, to the north the Lluta River estuary which 'good for nothing' Peruvians had left an infected swamp and Chile had drained. We looked out at the ocean that extended north-west beyond Easter Island, beyond Micronesia, weeks away by ship to the nearest mainland, China's Guangdong Province.

Gonzalo said, 'With her deep-sea port and huge estuary, Arica is our city most vulnerable to tsunami. "Arica Forever" could prove to be terrible hubris.'

Bernard took Gonzalo's arm and broached a different subject. He had discovered that Arica possessed a church designed by Gustav Eiffel, which had been prefabricated in France and transported to Chile. Eiffel liked to be complimented on the bridges he'd built and to play down his too-famous Tower; he was hardly known as a church builder and Bernard was curious to see this rare example.

Gonzalo looked none too pleased, citing our schedule, but his misgivings were ignored. 'Just five minutes, in and out,' insisted Bernard. On the way, Gonzalo explained that the church had originally been intended for a town in southern Peru, and had been paid for by Peruvians. The ship bringing it from France docked at Arica but, by then, Peru and Chile were at war. When the war ended, the Aricans, who had no church, kept the one intended for Peru. The only known case of God's house being hijacked.

The town centre was quiet and our driver brought us within reach of the building. We turned a corner and were confronted by a high-roofed neo-Gothic building with big pointed windows on a solid iron framework. It was a model edifice of its vintage but, in that context of wooden shops and stucco offices, it looked like a hawk among sparrows.

We entered the well-lit interior. Bernard dipped a finger in the holy water font, crossed himself and knelt, his head bowed. We walked slowly up the main aisle to the Communion rail where Gonzalo drew our gaze up to the iron vaulting.

There was the sound of hurried footsteps behind me, then confusion. A sack was thrown over Gonzalo's head; two men grabbed him from behind the arms and frog-marched him down the aisle where a third man emerged from behind a pillar, pistol in hand and snarled, '*Que nadie se mueva!*' As the group neared the door, the gunman followed walking backwards with his pistol trained on us. Moments later they were gone and we heard the screech of tyres of a car pulling away.

We ran back to our driver and told him to dash to the police station. There we found the chief of police: sturdy, clean shaven, with quick eyes and strong chin. His jacket had frayed cuffs but was unstained, his trousers held a sharp crease and his ankle boots were polished, a far cry from the stock Latino sluggard of Anglo-Saxon fiction. He knew Gonzalo and immediately called the airport, the army post on the road up to Peru, then sent a policeman down to the port.

'These are not locals. Here we shout threats but draw the line at armed abduction.'

We stood waiting, feeling like absolute fools, out of our depth, Bernard clenching and unclenching his hands, doubtless angry with himself for having insisted on visiting the church. This act of brute force made our attempt to comprehend the land of Chile seem misplaced, even irresponsible. There was truth in the maxim that harsh lands breed violence.

Five minutes passed, then another five. We feared the worst. Those torture scars, the decision to go to law, his enemies thought nothing of kidnapping. Half an hour passed and it seemed like an hour. Then the phone rang: a call from the port. Señor Gonzalo found – unharmed. Suspicious characters were seen boarding a speedboat. In a shoot-out with coastguards Gonzalo had managed to slip away. The thugs had raced off to the safety of Peruvian waters.

Minutes later Gonzalo joined us, out of breath and looking strained. He asked for a hot coffee and brandy. We were impatient to hear his account and, with some reluctance, he explained.

'When we were in Calama I received a message from my lawyer. Was I going to testify against four Chilean nationals now seeking asylum in Argentina? When I agreed, he told the court I would be present next Monday. The news spread. Without me to testify, the case would be dropped. Hence our three hired thugs.'

I asked what the charge was.

'Misuse of copper wire,' he replied sardonically.

Bernard and I exchanged grim looks. We had read about attempts to bring torturers to justice which had resulted in members of the prosecutor's family being kidnapped and held for ransom. 'Will you carry on?' asked Bernard.

'After Pinochet, Chile needs to redeem her good name. That matters much to me. But is it really more important than my family's safety? I can still change my mind… Two days from now and I'll have to decide.' With an effort, he now struck a cheerful note. 'Forget about all this. We have a very interesting drive ahead.'

Once in the car, having disentangled ourselves from police processes, I thought about how there were now two momentous decisions to be taken by my travelling companions before we reached the end of our journey. Bernard's would influence the future of medical research into leukaemia while Gonzalo's could affect his country's standing in world opinion. These were difficult enough decisions to take in the calm of one's home. How much more so in wild and alien territory.

CHAPTER ELEVEN

Reverse Magnetism

From Arica we drove east to the fertile Azapa valley. Here were smallholdings separated by bushes and scrawny poplars, with homes made of disparate planks of wood and corrugated roofs. On the eastern side of the narrow valley the land soon sloped up to hills of arid scrub. On one bare slope, we were surprised to see patterns and figures. We turned off onto a track that gave us closer access. Dark stones had been set over light-coloured soil in squares, rhomboids and ovals amid five pin-men figures, one with outstretched limbs atop a tall pole. The largest design looked like a partly uncoiled rope ending in a hook enclosing a smaller rope and hook. All were composed of hard stones firmly embedded in a hard sand surface.

About their meaning, Gonzalo confessed his ignorance leaving us to proffer guesses. Were the Molle tribesmen who fashioned them around AD 700 making a declaration equivalent to 'Arica Forever'? Did the rope pattern represent the life-giving Azapa, winding out of the mountains? Were the pin-men signalling to their gods to take notice of them? Or was the jumble of images just a form of play, such as children draw with spades at the seaside? As we floundered into wilder speculation Bernard said seriously, 'Suppose we're responding to the tribe's secret intention, of inveigling passers-by to share their view of the world as a crazy, undecipherable hodge-podge?' It was uncharacteristic and I teased him. 'Still upset by the headlong collision of tectonic plates?'

Gonzalo told us that Chile had 125 geoglyph sites, a few of which were readily decipherable. One group depicts a large herd of llamas, others show schematized humans, some on rafts; there are big fish and geometric forms, notably stepped rhomboids, known as the Andean Cross and emblematic of the Tiwanaka culture of AD 600-1000.

'These traces give us a glimpse of the various tribes of the Andes region and their different ideologies. They remind us of all the cultures about which we know nothing because they left behind no written evidence. If only they had left a key to their languages, as the Egyptians did, we might come to understand these signs, and know these tribes as people.'

We continued skirting the Azapa River and the earth became more impoverished as the terrain steepened. We stopped at a checkpoint and Gonzalo hurried in to the police hut, emerging quickly to shout that he would be held up and we should go to the café up the road.

The small bar proved to be an appendage of the highway, serving parched long-distance truck drivers, while the cluster of houses nearby belonged with the river. The river emerged from a cascade bursting out from rocks to lay down a thin sandy sediment on the flat bed. On the poor ground we saw stubble of harvested maize, beside it rows of scraggy beans and root vegetables. Across the road stood the small windowless church, locked and disaffected. Its sacred purpose was now apparent only in the burial ground lying in its shadow. A bolster of dusty sand marked the lie of each occupant, seventy or so, most as anonymous as molehills. Here and there, sticks tied crosswise had blown down and disintegrated. Two bore the names of men, one aged forty-two, another forty-five. The struggle to wrest food from a grudging soil had snapped their lives in half. They had wrestled with the earth and earth had won. A body gnarled by digging, scything, threshing served as its own crucifix and the dust heaped over each shallow pit was itself a blessing.

Wretched mementoes spoke of those who grieved. One mound was covered by the top of a packing case as if to provide reposeful shadow or perhaps even to hint at a catafalque. Here the base of a plastic bottle held a desiccated branch; there flowers which had crumpled into dust were proffered in a bottle labelled Crystal. I remembered the crystal vase holding lilies on my parents' tomb, but this Crystal was the name of a popular beer and empty save for the tenderness it evoked.

There was sudden activity on the highway. A white car appeared at speed from the direction of Arica. The driver stopped outside the police post, dashed into the building and a minute or less later ran back and drove off fast up the mountain road.

There was no sign yet of Gonzalo so we sat down to soft drinks at the bar. The owner had the high cheekbones and slanting eyes typical of the Incas of Peru. His hands looked arthritic and he had trouble unscrewing the bottle tops. In answer to our query he explained that the white car belonged to a paramedic who had been summoned by the police post to attend to a crash or fatal accident higher up the road towards Bolivia.

'So you visited our *cementerio*?' he asked rhetorically. 'The bodies are buried with the little they have of finery and value: women with their earrings, necklaces and rings, men with a few silver coins.'

'Why is that?' I asked.

'My guess is they want to look their best when they arrive in Heaven. As though to say, "Maybe we're poor but we're by no means destitute."' After a pause, he resumed gloomily. 'Now youths from Arica – bad place – come to the graves with metal detectors and dig up the valuables. That's why the police station's been moved next to the church.'

Gonzalo hurried into the café and told us we'd be leaving at once. To avoid the accident which might block the highway, we'd follow the old mountain road.

I had left Chuqui mine with the sense that there was hope for Chile's harsh land. But now this was effaced by the stunted maize, the crumbling cemetery and the reports of its defilement. As we edged our way, caterpillar-like up the twisting dusty road with a sheer drop below, the rugged mountain lost its awesome grandeur for me. I saw it as an obese overgrown bully, one of a hideous gang that had shouldered out all but a mite of arable soil near the river.

At each rabbit-leg turn, our offside wheels came within two fingers' breadth of the void. Taking such a road so soon after the shock of kidnap called for unusually strong nerves and a fierce determination to show us what he had promised. Only his white knuckles betrayed the strain Gonzalo was feeling.

As we climbed, the noise of the straining engine became muzzier and only when we were halfway down our cautious descent did a click in my ears signal clear hearing.

We rejoined the highway which followed the river's course. The gradients were easier and the road was now wide enough for two vehicles but blind corners could hide one of the many Bolivian trucks stacked high with hardwood for export by sea. Gonzalo was relaxed enough to name the trees that looked like pine but were really beech; he pointed out a sandwiched shelf of sedimentary rock and said it was a part of Chile's coastline thrust up by continental collision.

The road steepened, its offside falling away to scattered rocks. Gonzalo slowed so that we could see a rough cross wedged in the rocks made of two Bolivian plates nailed together.

'Two trucks collided head on. Both drivers died.'

'The cross marks their grave?'

'No, it's just a memorial. They were buried in their home towns… Trucks are often overloaded and then their brakes give.'

The abduction of Gonzalo, the accident that had made us take the rugged diversion and now this. Bernard would be invoking St Christopher.

We had reached fairly level ground with hills rising on either side when Gonzalo stopped the car at a barely visible line of white paint beside the road. He told us all to get out and look at the lie of the road. Ahead looked level but the stretch we had just covered sloped gently upwards. The car was positioned at the beginning of the slope, facing downward. Gonzalo put the engine into neutral, released the handbrake, shut the door and asked us to watch closely.

He had promised surprises but we were quite unprepared for what followed. Very slowly and beyond the least doubt, our heavy vehicle was edging slowly up the hill backwards.

I stared in puzzlement, doubting my eyes. But the wheels were turning, the motor was silent and we had the benefit of full sunshine. Gonzalo paced the car and, ten metres up the slope, he pulled on the hand brake. He was enjoying our shock.

'How's that for defiance of inertia and gravity?'

'The road may look like it's climbing, but it can't be,' I objected stubbornly.

'The gradient's been carefully measured with a spirit level. Close on two degrees. See for yourselves. Stand by the car, then run backwards up the road and see what you feel.'

We did just that. Instead of puffing we found it easy going, as though a breeze was helping us along.

Mystified, we pressed Gonzalo to explain but he kept us dangling.

'Here's a clue. Some years back, a friend of mine noticed the needle on his compass dancing a samba. He realized that ferrous rock might lie in those mountains. Then a mining prospector got interested. He scanned the ground from a helicopter and registered a high level of iron, but too deep for profitable extraction.'

Gonzalo glanced up at the sun, then at the angle of the shadow cast by our car and then pointed out the ferrous area. 'The road runs north-east to south-west and the car moved back towards north-east. So the magnetic pull must come from further up the hill and slightly to the east.'

Then he pulled out his ace of spades. 'In fact, the iron-rich rock lies north of the road, facing towards the front of the car.' He pointed in the opposite direction to the escarpment.

'But from there the magnetic force would pull the vehicle down the slope.'

'Exactly – if they were normal magnetic rocks, but they're not. The magnetic field can, so to speak, change sex. You know how that was discovered?'

'In the Geneva synchrotron?'

'No… An Australian geology student was pottering around in the Outback. He stumbled on embers and stones arranged for cooking. An aborigine camp? Dedicated student that he was, he sketched his find and brought the embers back to his tutor. Carbon dating showed the embers to be 3,000 years old. The stones turned out to be lava with traces of iron and, when lava cools, iron filings line up to face north, but these had lined up facing *south*. It followed that 3,000 years ago, Earth's magnetic field was the reverse of what it is now. Since then, we've found that it has switched north-south-north-south many times in the past millions of years and no one yet has explained why.'

'Did the Almighty get bored?' I asked stupidly. 'Or get cramp in his right arm and switch to his left? Or enjoy watching swallows migrate to a chilly Arctic winter?'

'No, it's simpler than that. Our car moved backwards uphill because iron ore with a reversed magnetic field was pulling it. But we've yet to find an explanation for how or why the change of direction occurs.'

'So much the better,' I said. 'It remains a marvel.'

Bernard was shaking his head. 'You mean a mystery.'

'Same thing.'

'Not quite. Mystery implies that it's beyond man's powers to explain and, if that is the case, then magnetic reversal is one in the eye for geologists.'

Gonzalo made a show of being piqued. 'Not unlike the cuckoo and the platypus: dropped stitches in the loom of nature. These anomalies puzzle us and make us feel humble.'

'Or are they little jokes? Signs that even Jupiter can laugh?'

Gonzalo threw me an austere look. 'Magnetism is too elemental a force to laugh at. Earth's magnetic field is probably due to a dynamo that produces electric currents in the outer liquid part of its core, but we're not even sure about that.'

'The how and why remain unanswered,' said Bernard.

CHAPTER TWELVE

Dating the Andes

We climbed back into the performing car and continued climbing, higher and higher, meeting only the occasional truck. Steep escarpments on either side hid any view of the Andes. After a boring hour we pulled in at a truckers' stop, a café much like a minimalist stage set. Wooden frame, metal roof, a counter of heaped stones with behind it three crates of beer and a petrol stove.

Gonzalo ordered mugs of *maté de coca* with dried leaves off the coca bush, an evergreen akin to holly. We seated ourselves at a plank table on trestles. Opposite a trucker sipped his beer in weary silence. Buff skin, flat cheekbones and narrow slanting eyes, possibly Bolivian.

Bernard said the road had taken him back in time. 'Like riding on our *Montagnes Russes* – what you call a roller coaster. Every upswing of a loop, that sinking feeling in your stomach.'

'So you were feeling seasick!'

'Not at all. The sea lurches, this plunges. Tell me, why do people queue to experience risk when every cell in our body works flat out to keep us from risk?'

'It's odd,' conceded Gonzalo. 'Still a roller coaster is self-contained whereas our road has to follow the mountain's every contour. It reshapes the mountain, changing it from a barrier into a passageway. Our road builders fought the mountain with bare hands, picks and shovels. No explosive, no machines. Out of randomness, they carved purpose. They linked these isolated regions into one governable whole. You could say road builders created Chile. Their victory matches Trafalgar or Austerlitz. One day I'd like to put up a statue to commemorate all those nameless workers.'

He spoke with such earnestness that I felt, more than ever, that my reactions were too self-centred – and superficial. I must try to do better, I told myself.

Our mugs of steaming coca infusion arrived. Gonzalo said the *maté de coca* helped combat mountain sickness and pressed us to drink it.

As we were now approaching the proto-Andes, Gonzalo was curious to know what the idea of mountains evoked in us. Bernard said he'd been ski-ing one winter in the Alps when he saw slope crumble into avalanche, burying a line of climbers in thirty seconds. He'd also happened to be in Geneva's cathedral when Mont Blanc staged a Wagnerian drama of thunder and forked lightning. 'Mountains are danger zones that induce melancholy,' he concluded.

I followed with an account of a school climbing trip. 'Lakeland is a complex of tight little sheep farms separated by dry-stone walls, five-barred gates, copses and ditches. At ground level all you see is a series of self-contained units shut off from one another. But once we'd puffed our way up the mountain, all the separateness disappeared. A whole swathe of country came together and what we saw was like an immense mosaic floor. Elevation revealed the unity of the landscape and opened my horizons.'

I pressed Gonzalo for his feelings about mountains.

'They give me a strong sense of freedom. For Chile they are invaluable as frontiers.'

'Between earth and heaven?'

'Between nations. We face Argentina along 3,000 kilometres, Bolivia along 500. We'd need a huge army to defend that line. But mountains do it for us. The Andes are more precious than Chuqui's copper.'

Gonzalo emptied his mug. I sipped my infusion but Bernard left his untouched. 'What about your medicine?'

He made a dismissive gesture. 'At this height the water won't have boiled.'

We bumped back onto the highway. The route climbed slowly, hugging the curves of the river bed to where rock yielded to scrub then to grass slope. Animals strange to us came into view.

Bernard focused his binoculars. 'Llamas?'

'Their forebears. Wild *guanaco*, indigenous to Chile.' He reminded us that we had encountered them already in Patagonia where they were hunted by the Ona tribe. A small herd of the oddest-looking animals veered gracefully away from us. This creature was like a child's drawing of a deer with a lumpy trunk and overlong neck. Yet it moved gracefully on thin legs, the group suggestive of a ballet chorus. When, from a distance, they stopped to look us over, balancing fear with curiosity, I found them endearing. The more so when I learned that the guanaco is a wild species that not even the Incas managed to tame.

We left the car and, at a sign from Gonzalo, the driver slowly edged his way towards the herd, a coiled lasso on his shoulder. A dozen metres from the closest guanaco, he sent the cord spinning to alight around the animal's neck. Then he pulled in the slack.

We closed on his catch and ran our hands over the creature's rich tawny pelt with a smell of wool grease, patting its neck reassuringly. The eyes ceased to roll and the ears flattened by fear again lifted jauntily. Gonzalo looked proud and proprietorial whilst Bernard seemed pleased to have left behind inanimate havoc for the flow of life in unfamiliar form. I marvelled that so large a ruminant should make its home in scanty terrain.

Gonzalo rattled off essential facts. 'Life span fifteen years, one young after eleven months' gestation. Male dominated. A dozen females herd together with one male. The coarse wool pelt moults in summer and is used for blankets and rugs. The herd defecates in one spot and the dung is collected for fuel.' He went on to explain that the guanaco resisted domestication. Fossil evidence suggested it originated in North America's savanna as a camelid no bigger than a hare. High foliage obliged it to strengthen and lengthen its neck and the neck had remained pronounced despite there being no foliage at all in the Andean Altiplano because it provided biting and fighting power.

'Who is its enemy?' I asked.

'The puma. It catches the small young and the old. Most elude it and flourish. There's no other pressure. No competition for grass, therefore adequate food. None of the supposed struggles has forced it to change. Yet it *has* changed.'

Gonzalo explained that the number of red blood cells in guanaco living at sea level was approximately three million per microlitre. To survive at an average 3,000 metres altitude, the mountain guanaco required four times as many, so the blood samples show.

'Take a smaller species, the *vicuña*. It lives at even higher altitudes than the *guanaco* and needs fifteen million red blood cells. Its domesticated descendant, the *alpaca*, living even higher, has twenty million. And to survive extreme cold, it produces a much thicker pelt, the inner layer more like human hair than wool. All these changes were effected not in answer to competition or food shortage, but to altitude and temperature.'

'You're suggesting that Darwin got it wrong?'

'He adopted a mistaken theory. Malthus noted that England's poor had a high death rate because they reproduced fast and could not afford a healthy diet. Malthus's theory held good for the sudden doubling of numbers in industrialized England. But Darwin applied it lock, stock and barrel to the whole range of animal life in the wild. Here at least the conditions are the exact opposite.'

Bernard was looking at the male of the herd. 'No horns, no antlers. Do they have any means of defence?'

Gonzalo said they could give a nasty bite and a kick could sever a tendon. Darwin shot them for meat.

'And early settlers likewise? So how have they survived?'

'Because of their wool. Indispensable to the Indios for warm clothing. If you kill a guanaco, you get one clip of wool, but if you leave it to live out its time, you get ten.'

'What you're saying is that man defended the guanaco, so ensuring his survival and theirs.' Bernard fell silent, closed his eyes and pressed his chin in deep thought.

We resumed our journey and came to an out-jutting rock from where we expected to see a regular line of mountains rising northwards to the sharp peaks of the High Andes. What we saw instead was a battlefield extending in all directions, gutted as though by continuous shelling, bombing and landmines. All frozen motionless, silent and ominous. No life, not a blade of grass, all dismal grey.

'You look dismayed. But you needn't be!' said Gonzalo gleefully. 'This desolation is an indispensable early stage in the formation of the High Andes. You can see how the shock of converging tectonic plates disrupts Earth's rocky mantle on a massive scale. Rain and snow melt erode the pristine rock and make it look even more ruinous.'

He picked up a fine-grained dark-grey rock with relatively large crystals of white tabular feldspar and passed it to us for examination. This was andesite, so named because it is commonly found in the Andes. The crystal has a sixty per cent silica content and is formed out of lava from andesite volcanoes.

Realizing that the rock's constituents meant little to us, Gonzalo directed us to a huge recess in the landscape. The eroded basin looked about twice as wide as the Chuqui opencast mine and three times as deep.

'Can you see a tiny green spot at the far end?' he asked. Bernard found it with difficulty and passed the binoculars to me.

'That is a small field of cultivated maize or wheat. One family manages to eke out a living there. You see how Chileans never admit defeat!'

Given the extent of this rocky battlefield, I could focus only on one small part at a time, enough to realize that the loveable language of Earth that I knew, of geoglyphs spelling out harmony, here lay sprawled in unintelligible gibberish. I was filled with the sadness of Messiaen's *Quartet for the End of Time.*

Bernard grasped the binoculars, anxious to read the smallest detail. His attention was caught by a flat-topped ridge. 'It looks like a man-made shelter.'

Gonzalo nodded. 'It's a *pulcara*, a stone fortress built by Inca invaders a thousand years ago.'

We considered this lone weathered relic of man's activity, his age-long struggle for territory extending even to wilderness.

'A thousand years ago the Inca were the most advanced people of South America. They used gigantic blocks of stone to build imposing houses and temples, they domesticated and bred llamas and created an efficient postal service for governing their conquests. From Cusco, their mountain capital in Peru, they marched down through this wilderness, building fortresses along the way. They overcame all resistance and imposed an oppressive regime, forcing their subjects to work for them for three months of each year. They disarmed the Araucanians and took over their gold mines. From the Mapuche they grabbed the best part of their land. Even today the Mapuche use the word *huinca* as a deeply scornful term for stranger and robber.'

Gonzalo described how, after five hundred years of occupation, the Inca dominions shrank as soldiers were recalled to Peru. Their garrisons declined steadily. This, then, was the situation Valdivia encountered in 1540. The downtrodden tribes welcomed him and his soldiers as a shield against the Inca. Valdivia struck a deal with the Araucanians whereby he received a share of their gold mines, and the Mapuche were granted sanctuary on the island of Chiloé.

Gonzalo broke off suddenly as if exasperated with the vagaries of human greed. He was much more drawn to the eternal truths of chemistry and physics. He explained how the study of radioactive minerals like Rubidium 87 meant that the mountains we saw looming ahead could be given an age. Since radioactive minerals are heavy, they belong near to Earth's core but they may be forced upwards into mountain-building rock by heat and explosion. The number of radioactive atoms in Rubidium 87 declines at a fixed rate over time, changing into atoms of the isotope Strontium 87. Once the number of Strontium atoms is established, geologists can work back to when there were only atoms of the undecayed parent element and so the mountain as a whole can be dated.

Bernard was not convinced. 'But what if a random meteorite carrying rubidium and other heavy elements crashed down onto Earth's surface? That would skew your results and make the Andes appear millions of years younger.'

Gonzalo made a face. 'Very unlikely.'

Chile Rediscovered

'But possible. That's why I think scientists who air general theories based on unverifiable evidence are indulging in science fiction. We biologists are just as bad.'

I was on a different tack. 'So what can you tell us about the age of Chile?'

'Earth's original land mass split into continents 200 million years ago. Following the collision of the Peru-Chile plate, the main Andes *cordillera* began to form twenty million years ago, and the Andes as we see them here, eight million years ago.'

'Eight million!' I gasped.

'Strontium is as accurate a measure as the quartz in your watch.'

'Humbling figures!'

'What do you mean?'

'Geological time set beside the span of a man's life.'

Still in contrary mood, Bernard raised a cautionary hand. 'Hold on. The human body is also built in vast denominations. Your body comprises three trillion hard-working cells. That's three million million million cells, many times more than Earth's age in years. Every single cell is replaced by a new one every seven years and the code in all those cells is passed on to a new generation by chromosomes. Accumulations of rock through twenty million years is child's play compared to the combined cellular activity of the five billion people now on earth.'

Gonzalo sidestepped Bernard's gratuitously competitive claim by declaring boldly, 'The longer I study the lifespan of mountains, the more I find randomness, not to say incompetence. But I cannot believe in an incompetent creator.'

'You don't have to,' I said. 'You can date these proto-mountains by looking at the presence of Strontium. If God made that possible, then He wished us to date mountains. Equally, dating should not be used to fault God's creative acts.'

In any case, it seems to me that there is no paradox: having decided on matter's general direction and development, God allows the specific processes to occur helter-skelter, in haphazard ways.'

'God is not to be found in limited research findings and half-truths,' said Bernard. 'It would be foolish to expect a "quick fix" of the universe tailored to man's pathetically short life and limited intelligence. What right have you to claim that *Genesis* tells us the truth about God? As a geologist, you are also necessarily a historian. Please, let's look at *Genesis* in its historic context.'

'Of course. You go ahead.'

'In or around 800 BC, when Homer's gods were locked in family quarrels and not above starting the Trojan War, when Babylon's many gods dwelt two years' stormy voyage away from Earth, aloof from mankind and rejecting out of hand a hero's plea to be granted eternal life …'

'But didn't at least one of their gods dwell in Babylon?' I interposed.

'Yes, Ishtar, goddess of love, in fact a much-feared nymphomaniac who took sadistic pleasure in seducing the city's youth. Into that cruel world blazed *Genesis* like a comet. In language simple and clear it stated: there is one God only, not many, and He is the opposite of aloof, in fact loving and beneficent. By any reckoning, this must be the most original declaration ever, for it has no known antecedents.'

Gonzalo objected that the first three chapters of *Genesis* were nothing more than a fairy tale, to which Bernard retorted that they were historical fact, like so much of the Old Testament.

'After treating cosmology historically, *Genesis* describes the creation of mankind. If you treat this as purely imaginative, you ignore certain important truths. In his goodness, God wishes to create a man in his own likeness and a woman also.

113

That creation is made not from Earth nor from the array of animals previously created and listed in *Genesis*, but solely from the likeness of God. God then breathes a moral conscience into Adam and Eve by means of which they know what they do when they eat the forbidden fruit. And God gives them knowledge of how to make children thus ensuring the propagation of man.

'Having created Adam, God speaks to him several times. This means Adam could understand what God was saying because he was created with a knowledge of God's language implanted in him.'

Here I interrupted. 'God did not always use his own language. When speaking to Moses, he used Moses's language and the Ten Commandments were conveyed in Hebrew. After the collapse of the Tower of Babel, the whole world had different languages so the language of God as spoken by Adam and Eve was lost.'

'Consider the six days of Creation,' resumed Bernard. 'A pastoral people 1,800 years before Christ possessed a rich oral history which they counted in generations as they lacked words for very long stretches of years. When trying to indicate the successive work of God, the most resonant idea of time was the word denoting man's working span between dawn and dusk: Day. Day was so immediate a concept as to be readily understandable as a metaphor for an incalculable period of time.'

I suggested that the six days should be read in the context of what immediately follows: God's gift of life to the first man and woman plus the further gift of happiness on the pristine Earth symbolized by a garden.

'So the end purpose of six days' creation is mankind, made in God's image therefore possessed of free will and *beneficentia*. *Genesis* is as much about the present as the remote past. What other reading of man on Earth has rivalled it?'

'Islam,' I replied.

'But Islam is based on the *Old Testament* God, same as the God of the Jews who venerated mountains as evidence of God's enduring and fearsome power. But in the *New Testament*, mountains become quiet places for communicating to the crowd. One of Christ's teachings measures the crowd against the mountain: if a man has sufficient God-given faith, he will be able to uproot this age-old mountain and set it down in the sea. Christ is telling the crowd that God can make free with the laws and regularity of nature if it serves His purpose. That can also apply to how and when the Andes became the great range of mountains we see before us.'

Gonzalo had been listening with growing anxiety. Perhaps he was controlling his urge to disagree with Bernard or perhaps it was just his usual clock-watching. 'We're running late!' he exclaimed. 'We'll make it up on the drive down.'

The phrase struck me as funny and I laughed aloud. Gonzalo stared at me, then he too laughed with relief. He was back in control of the situation and could rein us in with his reading of chasms, gullies and invisible streams.

'When the sharp edges of those distant peaks are weathered away, clay and grit washes down to more temperate zones where organisms contribute humus, the raw material of soil: the mountain becomes an intimate part of man's world.'

He pointed to a wide area of sloping rocks. 'These are the epitaph of a lost and forgotten river, rising high in the Andes and potentially as powerful as the Azapa. Our engineers have plotted its course and plan to divert it to the coast. We will harness it to a new copper mine, which is already on the drawing board and which will be bigger than Chuqui. The flow of water will generate flows of foreign currency.'

CHAPTER THIRTEEN

The Song of the Mountains

At our next pit stop we watched a Peugeot pull up with a screech of tyres. We had not seen a private car since leaving Arica. Out jumped a couple in their early twenties, wearing ski clothes and trainers. They limbered up and began to perform a series of stretching exercises.

When they came to the trestle bar for *maté*, I asked where they were from.

'Vancouver. We're doing a post-graduate course in economics.' Knapsacks, climbing boots and ropes were visible in the back of their car. The man said they were heading for Parinacota, a 6,000 metre volcano near the Bolivian frontier.

'Vancouver's near the Rockies, yes?' asked Bernard, still in querulous mood. 'Why travel halfway across the globe to climb a comparable slab of rock?'

The Canadian frowned. 'Nothing comparable. Parinacota's a real bastard. Capricious and two-faced. Up to every trick in the game. He'll lure you on with blue sky and a light breeze. Within sight of the summit, he'll blind you with dense mist, then batter you with a blizzard, maybe an avalanche. We found that out last year.'

'Mike suffered frostbite,' put in the young woman; 'three toes of his left foot had to be binned.'

116

'Parinacota thought he'd seen the last of me. Now I'm back to show him who wins.'

'Parinacota conquers you or you conquer him… Is that how you see it?' I asked.

'Guess so.'

Mike's demonization of the mountain prompted Gonzalo to tell us of the Incas' terror of dangerous peaks. Recently an international team of mountaineers and archaeologists had climbed the summit of Cerro Llullaillaco, nearly 7,000 metres, one of the Andes' highest. There they came on a stone and gravel platform covering the frozen body of an Incan ritual sacrifice, a boy of about seven years old. Later the team unearthed two more frozen sacrifices, both eight-year-old girls in perfect condition, one of whom had a charred ear, shoulder and chest. She had been tied to a stake just as a thunderstorm approached and her body struck by lightning. The Incas would have rejoiced: the mountain had accepted their offering.

The Canadians seemed more than ever determined to get to the top. We said goodbye and wished them success.

'What's your assignment?' the woman asked me.

'Just at present, wondering.'

'Wandering?'

'Bit of both.'

She raised her eyebrows, puzzled. 'Stay on the map,' she announced gaily.

Bernard and I exchanged a look. Our exploration seemed tame in comparison with what these Canadians had set themselves. They needed to attribute a grim personality to the mountain in order to drive themselves on. It was plainly unreasonable but necessary to strengthen the will.

We were still dawdling when our attention was caught by a remarkable arrival: a middle-aged lady astride a she-donkey. We could make out layers of home-knitted sweaters, ankle-length

117

bootees, a pale blue scarf and a smart Chilean panama hat. She rode up to us confidently and said in Spanish, 'I am English. My name is Miriam Fairfield and I am conducting research into Amerindian languages. How much further to the Altiplano?'

She dismounted and led her donkey to a patch of scrub. We stared in fascination. Gonzalo introduced himself and explained we were studying the formation of mountains and the evolution of man from apes. Within minutes the conversation passed from Darwinism to Darwin's neglected contemporary and elaborator of evolutionary biogeography, Alfred Russel Wallace of whom she was a champion.

'Wallace's theory: he's sound,' she declared with conviction. 'He recognized the all-important role of language in the formation of society. But he didn't know what we know now, that apes lack the complex mechanism needed to produce the range of sounds needed for language.'

She paused, removed her hat and, with a half-smile, turned to each of us.

'My field is linguistics, but that doesn't mean I've learned, studied and compared a few of the two thousand languages spoken today. What I do is study the relationship between one language and the society that brought it to birth.'

'But how?' asked Gonzalo. 'That will have been thousands of years ago.'

'Take Wallace: he studied a backward Amazon tribe that had never been in contact with other tribes nor with the Portuguese. A much-used word in their limited language was "Devil". Death – any death, animal or human – was the Devil's doing. Their society had survived without the idea or the word for "God". A tribe can have a word for "Justice" and on that alone form a civilized society.'

'Can you really go as far as that?' Bernard cut in.

'Certainly. Think of the English today. A majority have

chosen to believe that God is dead – and that the Queen is out of date. Yet they're still respected worldwide for their system of justice.'

We were left baffled. Self-confident and friendly, Miriam Fairfield belonged to a long line of brave English female explorers with unorthodox views, exotic but familiar. Not one to waste time, she made to retrieve her donkey as Gonzalo gave her directions.

'A kilometre off the road you'll see a rough track up to your left. Follow that for a couple of hours and you'll reach the Altiplano.'

'*Hasta luego!*' she cried and off she trotted.

Gonzalo turned to me with a frown. 'She is right to say that justice is the basis of society. I have an obligation to see that my torturers are brought to justice.'

'Does that really follow?'

'I think so. For the sake of Chile's good name worldwide.'

He left it at that. It was time to go.

The road drew us away from the overwhelming steepness and followed the Lauca River upward. The scrub-covered banks were very soon obscured by low grey cloud and heavy rain. Gonzalo switched on the car lights and, hunched forward, peered not straight ahead but to the nearside: a slight thinning of greyness hinted at where the road fell sheer into a hundred metres of emptiness.

We broke free from the jolting bumpy track onto macadam and again began to climb steeply. Grass dwindled then faded out, leaving us in grey space and increasing cold. The mist gave no sign of lifting and visibility was down to three metres. 'Owing to power failure the star performance will not now take place,' I announced to myself in dismay. Bernard was moving his lips silently, probably praying. Worse and worse. Despite the heater, I was beginning to shiver and my brain had gone numb. I kept picturing the guanaco with its supercilious look. It knew that man had failed to adapt. On and on. Then suddenly, like a theatre curtain, the mist lifted.

Gonzalo turned to us with sudden animation. 'We're nearly in sight of the High Andes, known as the *cordillera*. The parallel ranges of the cordillera run the full length of South America and are one of the very few natural phenomena observable from space.'

We entered a level stretch of road where we stopped. Instead of the scattering of separate mountains I'd expected, I saw a massive continuum of rock bulking out and upward, defying every limitation as it blocked out the lower part of the sky and much of its afternoon light. Here and there, the rock peaked in a line of jagged asymmetrical crests, some piebald with patchy summer snow, all integral to the massive excrescence.

My eye was drawn to the skyline. The waves of irregularly spaced crests gave an impression of rhythm upon which I tried in vain to impose a pattern. I recalled Gonzalo explaining that high altitude is subject to continuous gusts of icy wind. Perhaps this was the key to a secret pattern. Just as the ultrasonic calls of whales pass through the seas, could it be that these crests transformed the icy wind into song? Even a small cavern will shout a reply to our whispered greeting. My musing thoughts turned to distant mountains. Perhaps such music had prompted the Psalmist to pen that startling call, 'Praise the Lord all mountains and hills.'

Praise for what? Could the mountains be urging us to recognize the strength and power of whatever or whoever had shaped our habitat? The sky and the air already made that plain but perhaps not enough. Sky was subject to diurnal change and seasonal transition whereas here was permanence, or at least its semblance scaled to our limited vision.

Gonzalo's reactions were less fanciful but just as wondrous.

'I've known these mountains since childhood,' he said warmly. 'What you see is the end product of geological processes, the positive and permanent result of millions of years of disruption, eruption and destruction.'

Bernard responded to my questioning glance. 'Gonzalo is right to describe Chile as a land ninety-two per cent absolutely barren, hence requiring continuous immense efforts from its people. Why this barrenness should be I've no idea. But maybe this is the wrong question.'

CHAPTER FOURTEEN

A Herdsman and his Llamas

The air was thin on the Altiplano, an extensive plateau 4,500 metres above sea level with its own sheltered climate between the two mountain chains. 'You must be relieved to be quit of what you termed "desolate chaos",' remarked Gonzalo with a wry grin.

In the space of a minute, as from an underwater dive, we had surfaced to sunlight and colour bursting upon us like a firework display. The air was clear and unclammy and the space felt three-dimensional. Only half-believing, we jumped out onto level ground covered with a thin layer of glossy green grass packed tight as watercress, interspersed with low bushes in leaf. Here was what had been missing for so long – we saw life. Small birds with bright yellow breasts, warblers, pippets and rust-coloured flycatchers darted through the thin air into the foliage. Further on, a scattering of llamas cropped the bristly grass watched by a herdsman.

I felt surprise, excitement, then relief, all in a rush. More was to come. The verdure sloped down to a lake clear as glass with a sun-flecked surface on which geese glided, trailing glistening fans of overlapping ripples. The scene was so quiet yet also dramatic and solemn, as when a Muslim bride is unveiled, radiant in colourful silk and aglitter with trinkets.

Bernard examined the geese and their houseboat reed nests that drifted on the surface while I knelt and sampled a palmful of water, sweet as from a spring. Gonzalo watched us unwrap our surprises.

Bernard indicated a goose with black plumage. 'You know what that means?'

'You've discovered a rare species?'

'It means bad luck.'

Now Gonzalo pointed out the form of Mount Parinacota in the middle distance, quite alone, pyramid-shaped, with its sides rising up to a flat summit. Snow on its upper half looked as if it was mediating between rock base and immense blue sky.

Since childhood I have delighted in finding out about birds and their nesting habits. Before flying to Santiago I had memorized all I could about Chilean birds and now I had a gala day with the many small variegated birds perching just long enough for identification. Species I recognized from my boyhood – finches, sparrows, wrens, flycatchers were here with exotic names. There was the black-hooded Sierra finch, here a rufous-collared sparrow, a woodpecker called an Andean flicker and a plain-brested earthcreeper with a long curved bill.

Gonzalo explained why they looked partly familiar. Perhaps as long as sixty million years ago, their ancestors had flown south from North America, which was then joined to Europe, before North and South America came together.

'I accept that Chile's birds are poor in number,' he continued, 'but each species is rare or unique. Take the condor. It's just a North American vulture with a scrawny neck and a taste for blood. It's too heavy to fly long distances so what does it do here? It nests in high canyons and glides on thermals to swoop down on nearby prey, like a defenceless newborn llama. No need for centuries of preferred mating. It's adapted at once like other animal species to our land and climate.'

Bernard turned to me in all seriousness and asked an odd question. 'How do you *see* birds?'

'As creatures with the truly wonderful gift of flight. The way poets see them: take Hopkins' lines: "dapple-dawn-drawn Falcon, in his riding of the rolling level underneath him steady air". And composers too: Saint-Saëns's piece *The Swan* lets you imagine the beautiful creature gliding just above the surface of a lake.'

'Why would your God have created birds?'

'Why not for mankind? For their beauty, to give us pleasure. They're models of home-building – and homing.'

'Poetic,' said Bernard. 'I'm not convinced. Obviously Darwin doesn't satisfy me either. Darwin claimed that birds were descended from reptiles and that changes in plumage and everything else were due to natural selection and randomness. Today's scientists would regard the issue as more complex and problematic. We live in the age of the gene and its potentialities.'

'The age of the gene will be much worse,' protested Gonzalo. 'We will end up as programmed robots.'

'By no means.' Bernard was quivering with excitement, as if he had just resolved the contradictions that had been troubling him. 'Consider early man. I'll go along with Wallace's theory in that early man evolved in two distinct phases: in the first phase, developing an ability to speak and communicate in language; and later, forming the ability to make choices. And *Genesis* bears this out: it names groups of animals God created as they were known in 1800 BC when He spoke to Abraham. These groups are meant to be seen as containing many potentialities, which is precisely what the gene achieves. When seed and egg merge in the uterus, everything is in place for the formation of an individual human being. Most importantly his brain, which will provide the data for him to make free choices. It is those choices that define the unique individual.'

Bernard's mixture of early man, *Genesis* and his own experience of pre-natal identity left us stranded. As we pondered his words, our eyes were drawn to the group of llamas ambling slowly close to the lake. I saw them as stage comedians in fawn pantaloons and dancing pumps but theirs was a harsh life. At this height, with only tough *ichu* grass to nibble, they survived on a knife edge.

'Like the chinchilla, the domesticated llama has a valuable pelt,' explained Gonzalo. 'The coarse wool is used for blankets, and the skin off the neck makes strong lassos. The dung is good for cooking fuel and the meat, though tough, is full of vitamins. As a pack animal, it can carry forty kilograms for a march of three weeks without drinking for five days at a stretch.'

'Surely ready victims for the puma?'

'No pumas at this altitude.'

Bernard had approached one of the group and was now massaging its neck. He studied its eyes, lifting the lids, then the ears and finally tried to open its mouth whereupon it retracted its head and spat half-chewed *ichu* into his face.

Bernard stepped sharply back, wiped his face and moustache clean and joined in our amusement.

'What about poachers?' I asked.

'A herdsman's sling can kill at forty metres. No poacher wants to take that risk.'

Turning to Bernard, Gonzalo said, 'the most remarkable aspect of the llama is how it has adapted to the Altiplano's low oxygen count and increased the number of red blood cells to twelve million per microlitre. The best humans can manage at high altitude is seven million.'

After cupping his hand for refreshment at the lakeside, the herdsman was now approaching us, unhurried. He proved to be taller and broader than a lowland Chilean and, according to Gonzalo, probably had no mixture of Spanish blood. This showed in the distinctive physiognomy of broad face with prominent cheekbones, fleshy aquiline nose and brown smallish almond eyes. Suggestive of an Amerindian though the narrow eyes hinted at an origin more remote still, the cold wastes of Siberia. Broad shouldered, he held himself very straight, wrapped in an ankle-length poncho and silence. Wind and sleet had grooved his face, giving him an austere stern look.

Gonzalo drew on a patchy knowledge of Quechua, but the herdsman made no move towards us. I pressed Gonzalo to tell us about the herdsman's way of life.

'This lake apart, water is scarce, so his thick woollen vest stays unwashed. Once in a while his wife will pick off the lice and he'll enjoy chewing them. His diet is potatoes and a goosefoot called quinoa, its seeds used like rice, its leaves like spinach. Llama milk he leaves to the foals. By barter, he acquires two essentials, salt and coca. On his belt is a woven pouch containing coca leaves mixed with burnt stalks of quinoa which neutralizes the acid in digestive juices, so increasing the coca's effect. He holds a wad on his inside cheek, letting it from time to time mix with his saliva.'

Bernard considered the diet short on calcium and magnesium, leading perhaps to swollen goitre.

'The area dispensary has iodine-based preventive on its shelves,' acknowledged Gonzalo. 'But it just gathers dust. Notice how he keeps his distance and his dour, uncurious look – not hostile, just an assertion of his self-reliance. He'll never set foot in our dispensary save to get aspirin for his wife's headaches. By keeping to themselves, the Amerindians guard their identity, remembering perhaps that, by mixing with Spaniards, whole tribes were wiped out by measles and tuberculosis with which their immune systems couldn't cope. This area was evangelized by Spanish priests. There's a baroque chapel nearby, richly decorated with paintings and statues but long since closed save for one service a year at Christmas. It was another medicine they preferred to do without.'

'But how can this man survive at 5,000 metres plus?' queried Bernard. 'Mountaineers can achieve seven million red blood cells per microlitre at 4,500 metres but, to reach that figure takes a month of adaptation and the count doesn't rise further. The change seems to be a response to air pressure, like mercury rising in a barometer.'

Gonzalo agreed that additional haemoglobin might play a part. 'But for me the main factor is the Amerindian's barrel chest. I believe they have bigger lungs than ours, protected by a larger rib cage. If so, a structural modification of the ribs has evolved, which implies mutation and the transmission of a favourable gene.'

'Has anyone carried out research on chest expansion?'

'Not to my knowledge. But a Canadian ornithologist found that black Andean duck have larger lungs than duck of the same family at sea-level. A mutation in birds: why not also in man?'

The herdsman had been showing signs of impatience and now took to flourishing a short stout stick in order to head his flock in the direction of the setting sun.

'Do you think he'd let me measure his chest?' asked Bernard.

'We'd have to offer a quid pro quo… I'll try.'

The Amerindian was reluctant to delay departure but Gonzalo's cajoling prevailed. He'd agree for some aspirin. Bernard had aspirin in his toilet bag and needed cord for the measurement.

'You'll find it under the dashboard. But hurry or he'll be gone.'

The car was some distance away on higher ground. Bernard trotted over, found what he needed and started running back. Twenty or so paces down the hill, he faltered: his head jerked back, his body spreadeagled, then crumpled and tumbled heavily. Shouting in alarm, we ran to where he lay, face down. Turned him on his back. Face colourless, contorted, mouth wide open, he was fighting for air. I unbuttoned his shirt collar while Gonzalo unpocketed a vial of ammonia which he held under Bernard's nostrils until it produced a spasm.

Pulmonary oedema can cause mental confusion, even brain damage, and Gonzalo was taking no chances. 'Behind the back seat, there's an oxygen kit. Fetch it and hurry.'

I ran over, found the kit and ran back. My heart was racing.

The next ten minutes would be crucial. I held a rubber mask over Bernard's nose and mouth while Gonzalo controlled the supply by adjusting the valve on the pint-sized oxygen cylinder. Very slowly he lowered the input and after ten minutes he removed the mask.

Bernard's breathing came in slow heaves: he was straining and still in shock. Perhaps I could get the chest measurements he wanted. Gonzalo nodded. I picked Bernard's pocket, found the cord and a foil of ten aspirin. As in the last shot of a Western, the herdsman and his stock were fading into the dusk.

I started to run, found myself short of breath, seconds later gasping for air, stopped and bent double, then fell on my knees. Minutes passed before my breathing returned to normal and by then herdsman and llamas had disappeared. I limped back to Gonzalo and Bernard feeling utterly useless.

Slowly, unsteadily, Bernard assumed a sitting position. 'Hypoxaemia,' explained Gonzalo. 'I've seen several such cases. There are no after-effects.'

'Help me.' We each gave Bernard a hand and, step by slow step, returned to the car sunk in our thoughts. Bernard had refused to drink *maté* and he'd been forewarned by the black goose yet he'd insisted on measuring the herdsman's lungs and to hell with his own.

I had pictured the worst: losing a new friend, his family's grief, the loss to medical science. I felt a wider *frisson*: lack of air was the Andes' deadliest weapon for it struck without being seen.

CHAPTER FIFTEEN

Shelter

Our mood was depressed and Gonzalo did not try to talk us out of it. So far he had stuck firmly to his tight programme, but now he decided to skip a visit to the Catholic mission chapel and instead head back for Arica.

We heard a growl of thunder, then its echo off rock. 'Storm to the south. That will slow us. Best be on our way.'

We seated ourselves in the car, Gonzalo at the wheel, each lost to his own thoughts. The party was due to break up soon and so much discussion was left unfinished. My belief that earth had been created for man to plough and sow had been lost, and neither the Andes nor its animals had provided Gonzalo or Bernard with evidence that might weigh with a reductionist. This encounter with mountain building had shown up our puniness, our near-nothingness in space and time. To fancy that such vast movements had been conducted with mankind in mind seemed hubris close to lunacy.

Lightning flashed but we saw no bolts. It was like stage lighting. Rain fell, gently at first, then clicking on the roof in the form of hail, thick as a café bead curtain. Our wipers couldn't keep pace and our driver rubbed off the blur from our screen while Gonzalo wiped the sweat off his brow. All of a sudden, the driver raised his left hand, signalling to Gonzalo that he was about to vomit and we stopped just in time.

Our road began to hug the ins and outs of a near vertical craggy mountain slope. Dynamite had slashed the almost sheer face and, above each open gash, a steel mesh was pinioned to check any haemorrhage of loosened rock. This had sometimes ripped away: snow melt once more victorious.

Rain acted like a dipper on our extra-strong beam. Bernard crossed himself and murmured a decade's worth of *Ave Marias.*

To reach Arica, we needed to clear the mountains before darkness closed in but to venture downward at much speed would be inviting serious trouble. We sneaked our way downhill in low gear, Gonzalo's eye picking out – or more often guessing – the road edge, ready to slam on the brakes at the slightest misjudgement.

Rain at this intensity was like hysterics – bound soon to cry itself out. Not once did Gonzalo complain. The difficulties built into Chile's terrain and climate formed part of his heritage.

With no warning, he braked hard, jolting us almost out of our seats. Gonzalo cut the engine and seconds later our ceiling light went out. Lifting his hands from the wheel Gonzalo exhaled, half-sighing, half-snarling: '*¡Qué mierda!* The words tore through his gritted teeth.

Our headlamps were dead, the wipers also and, through a rain-blurred screen, we could make nothing of whatever heavy obstacle we had struck head-on.

Gonzalo rummaged in the cubby hole, found a torch and went out to look. As he moved about, sizing up the damage, his torch beam showed in fits and starts that a rock fall had spilled onto the road. This was not loose rubble, but heavy boulders half the size of the car.

Gonzalo called me out and shone his light on the right front wheel skirting the macadam, a finger-length of tyre actually off the road, suspended like a suicide hesitating before the leap.

He examined our situation from every angle, then announced his plan. We'd retrace our route in reverse, with me guiding by the light of the torch. Some way back, we'd find the turn-off to a village where we'd spend the night.

He fetched a red reflective triangle from the back and set it up on the far side of the rock slip, steadying it with fragments of stone. Then he returned to take the driver's seat while I, holding the torch, walked behind the car and waited to hear the engine start.

This was a reversal in the most humbling sense, and we couldn't even grouse, aware that we might have ended as battered corpses eighty metres below, four more victims of natural disaster.

Slow and silent as a funeral march we edged our way back. The engine in reverse tended to hiccups and nudged the spare wheel into the small of my back. Ten minutes on, we encountered a second rockfall which narrowed rather than blocked our passage.

As the rain stopped it became noticeably colder. My fingers felt numb, my grip slackened and the torch wobbled in my hand. I thought longingly of the sweater in my holdall. The beam began to pale. More time lost, for I had to walk up and back the width of the road before instructing Gonzalo to back up further.

At long last we came to a turn-off, then a scattering of small homes and a small electricity generator. Dots of light from windows served as Gonzalo's guide as he threaded his way through an alley to a mud street of one-door, two-window house fronts capped with wrinkled iron and dimly lit by a lamp-post at the far end. He stopped at a house less small than the others and got out. A second rap on the door and a woman opened cautiously, let him in and closed the door again.

More waiting. Not satisfied with being alive, Bernard and I speculated on the possibility of food.

Presently we were summoned. The house had one big room lit by a single bulb hanging from the ceiling, clean cement floor, bare stucco walls and a scattering of half a dozen tables. The house served as a café and occasional overnight refuge for stranded truck drivers and mountaineers.

Gonzalo had disappeared behind a screened-off cooking area, soon to emerge carrying large cups of tea and hunks of white loaf, assuring us something hot would follow.

A corridor led to the owner's living room. She was *mestiza* – mixed race – a widow with no children. Another corridor led to a large patio behind the house, suitable for pack animals. Here Gonzalo used a short wave radio to alert the frontier garrison. Then he left to find the local official to arrange for him to clear the road at first light.

The *mestiza* had been heating up boiled potatoes and legs of tough chicken. We wolfed these down, grateful for the warmth they afforded. She turned on a cassette player: the music was banal but it helped to make the room feel less chilly.

We brought in our bags and arranged our kit in parallel lines on the cement floor. Our driver was still feeling unwell and had been granted the luxury of sleeping in the car. We were not yet ready for a night's rest and chatted about what we planned to do upon our return to Santiago.

From the corridor leading to the patio there suddenly emerged a bare-headed lady in bedraggled clothes. Miriam Fairfield! Without her panama hat, she was barely recognizable.

She looked us over and laughed. 'What have you been up to?' We told her about our accident. 'You should have chosen donkeys. They never let you down.'

She had ridden through the storm but had then decided to seek shelter. She had been directed to the *mestiza* who had offered her a bed for the night in her own room and her donkey was now feeding in the patio.

I asked her where she was headed on the Altiplano.

'I'm off to stay with a nomadic tribe.'

'Lucky you!'

She looked surprised. 'Most people think nomads should be avoided. Would you like to accompany me?'

I explained that we were travelling as a group and were due back in Santiago but that I would try to persuade Gonzalo to make a detour.

'Call him over now and let me speak to him. Or rather let him listen to the music I'm going to play.'

She took a cassette from her holdall and swapped it into the player. A fast beat, discreet drums and fifes as background to women's voices. This was joyful music and original also, played on apparently home-made instruments, shrill penny whistles and deep bassoons. Feminine music, women singing their contentment with a touch of pride.

'It's music and singing by the Aymara tribe, recorded by a missionary and donated to the Linguistics Institute. Doesn't it make you curious to visit them with me?'

I turned to Bernard. 'They're an Amerindian people. Like our herdsman this afternoon. You could measure their lung capacity…'

Bernard said he was interested, but he didn't want to risk another accident. The car had a damaged headlight.

Gonzalo was against altering our timetable. 'Our herdsman today was typical Amerindian, Miriam's tribe is Amerindian. I don't see why we should go there just because we like their music. Anyway I'm opposed to so many strangers descending on them, assessing their IQ and measuring their lungs. It's unfair and would give them a sense of inferiority.'

Miriam nodded. 'I appreciate what you're saying but I'm going to them humbly. They are the ones with a language richer and more precise than ours: I am the one who is learning and beginning to speak it correctly. The Aymara will be honoured if we go about it tactfully.'

Seeing she was not making any impression on Gonzalo and Bernard, she tried a new argument. She described how language was important as the medium by which we express character, love, our deepest thoughts and – though the word was unfashionable – our soul. 'In every language the presence or absence of a word for God is crucial. When Matteo Ricci, an Italian polymath missionary, arrived in China around 1600 he found that, although the Chinese had kept exact records of the planets, they had no word for God. Many peoples have no word for God yet they are open to the idea of Transcendence.'

'You could say the same about contemporary philosophy,' I remarked. 'Logical positivism is closed to Transcendence for the absurd reason that we cannot prove its existence scientifically.'

In the silence that followed we were each in our different way taken aback. This eccentric lady who hoped to ride all the way to the Altiplano on a donkey was determined to discover more about Gonzalo's beloved Chile than we had managed with geology, biology and history. But would she be likely to find out anything of importance about the Aymara with her school-taught smattering of their language? We were not meant to debate the question. Resuming command, Gonzalo announced we had five minutes to prepare ourselves for sleep. The generator was about to shut down and our single bulb would go dead.

With a brief 'thank you' to Gonzalo, Miriam was quick off the mark. Picking up her belongings, she hurried to the bedroom while the rest of us laid ourselves down on the concrete floor.

CHAPTER SIXTEEN

An Enigmatic Book

Next morning Gonzalo got up early and arranged for breakfast to include omelette for each of us. To compensate for his spoilsport attitude the previous evening, he told us the little he knew about the Aymara. They were quite unlike any other tribe, in fact a mysterious people. Any sensible tribe would long ago have shifted to a less exhausting climate. After centuries, they still refused to learn Spanish and many suffered from goitre but would not touch Western medicine.

He turned to Bernard. 'I doubt whether they'd allow their blood count to be taken. You'd be unable to explain in sign language that it wasn't the first step to drawing off all their blood.

'And there's a further mystery. They don't kill their animals for meat. Only when a llama reaches old age do they put an end to its life. Mercy killing. Yet meat would give them much-needed extra nutrients. Still, I have to admit that they do have some qualities. They leave their neighbours in peace, barter with them for food and play fair when exchanging goods. And they keep their animals pastured in their own territory.'

I was keenly interested in this curious combination of total withdrawal and fair dealing. While researching my trip, I had come across an abstruse book in Italian with the enigmatic title,

The Art of the Aymara Language. Why had he called it an artistic language?

Miriam joined us as our omelettes were brought in and we all gave our full attention to breakfast. Only then did I share my curiosity about the book subtitled: '*A Full Account of the Art and Grammar of the Aymara Language, with many varied ways of expressing one's meaning.*' The author was a Roman Jesuit – Father Ludovico Bertonio – based in Peru, and the volume was published in Rome in 1603.

'Bertonio gives examples of the different modes of expressing the same statement according to circumstance. He concludes that Aymara is an outstandingly precise and subtle language, geared to the person or persons one is addressing. He shows how particles can be inserted into verbs to create an exactness and truth not found in Greek, Latin or the Romance languages. Last thing you'd expect from a tribe living from hand to mouth.'

The book had taken Bertonio ten years to write and then a further nine years to publish a Spanish-Aymara dictionary. There was no evidence that he made even one convert to Christianity. He had presumably intended his books to be used by others, but the Aymara were never evangelized because their language was too complicated to learn.

'Perhaps Bertonio was aware that the Aymara would never succumb to conversion. He recognized that Aymara was an astonishingly complete and perfect language – beautiful too – else he would not have referred to it as a work of art.'

Gonzalo had been listening closely but now interrupted. 'What is the use of Bertonio's work since no one can speak Aymara?'

To which Miriam replied that she could speak it if only she could be sure her pronunciation was right.

Suddenly relenting, Gonzalo suggested that we could accompany her; he would make the necessary adjustments so that we could still meet our connections. He told us to pack while Miriam left instructions for her donkey's care during the fortnight she planned to stay in the Altiplano.

Gonzalo instructed our driver to walk to the nearest village and then take the battered bus to Arica. We were now ready to set off. There was no road and, taking his bearings by the rising sun, Gonzalo started off up an expanse of thin untrodden grass.

Miriam began telling me of the clarity she enjoyed in the Aymara language. She had studied agglutination. As in German, this makes for one long word, more precise than a long bunch of phrases. By combining two hundred suffixes with verbal roots, Aymara could produce one million different words.

'Here we have this perfect language, but we are forced to ask who made it. Evidently not the Aymara who, as nomadic herdsmen, lead a simple life and need only a simple language. Several explanations have been offered ever since Dante made Philology a serious subject of study. My answer, for what it's worth, turns on the Tower of Babel.'

This took me by complete surprise and I suggested we consult Bernard. 'He's frequently quoting *Genesis* and posing interesting questions.'

Miriam reflected before replying with a firm No. 'He may speak English but he does his thinking in French. That will muddle our conversation, which is going to be complicated enough.'

She paused and took a deep breath. 'According to *Genesis*, God created the first man with a soul. He must therefore have provided the first man with awareness of good and evil and how to choose between them. That required a method of reasoning which was logical and precise. This language was a one-off gift to man – until it was snatched away in the confusion of Babel and its elements scattered worldwide.'

She paused to assess my response. I was puzzled by her ability to convey so much so briefly, but also doubtful. 'So far I follow you. But from Babylon to the Altiplano? Surely that's impossible?'

'Not at all. Historians are generally agreed that the Amerindian peoples migrated from Siberia crossing the Bering Strait. My view is that they originally came from Babylon.'

We had passed only untrodden meagre grassland, but now Bernard cheered as he spotted a group of llamas and their herdsman.

'Early morning. Probably left his family on a week's migration – we can't be far off now,' said Gonzalo.

'Now's the time when my nerves will be tested,' said Miriam. 'I've never practised, and my speaking may be so garbled they won't understand a word.'

CHAPTER SEVENTEEN

The Tribe that Speaks
the Language of God

Gonzalo stopped the car well short of what appeared to be
a village, telling us that our watchword for the day was
Tact.

We shivered as we emerged into the cold air and strode out
towards the line of houses, sheltered with their backs to a rise
in otherwise flat grassland. Miriam announced that she would
go and talk to the women. She insisted on going alone,
explaining that her advances would be less effective with a
dumb man tagging along.

Most of the houses had a patch for growing vegetables,
mainly potatoes and goosefoot. Whilst mothers and small
children tended their crops, I felt free to inspect their houses.
Most were built of adobe with stones in the walls and flat coils
of clay for roofing. Windows and doors were very small and the
sombre interiors were decorated with bright pictures from old
magazines and calendars, years out of date. In villages higher
up the Altiplano, whole families probably slept and cooked in
a single room.

I caught glimpses of women of different ages working in
their homes or on their vegetable patches, all slim because
active. Their traits were familiar: oval faces with caramel
complexion, lively dark eyes and ample glossy black hair, often

plaited at the back. I saw no men at all – presumably absent on long journeys, finding pasturage for their animals.

All the women kept their breasts covered, wore ankle-length skirts, neat footwear and ponchos of bright primary colours which often accompany self-confidence. They were so busy in their work that they hardly noticed me. In some houses they were carding wool from alpaca and llama. We had seen the cloth they dyed and wove for sale on the roadsides. These women sang or hummed happily as they went about and their efforts were also evident in the general cleanliness: there was no litter in the pathways. In short, in all they did, they seemed quite unlike Chile's other tribes save perhaps the Mapuche who are practising Christians.

I was wondering where to go next when Miriam came to find me. She seemed pleased with her first encounters. They had found Miriam delightfully funny for wearing her usual trim panama, normally the prerogative of young married women whereas grandmothers were supposed to wear brown bowler hats.

I told her that I was curious to see inside a house but didn't want to offend the owner. Miriam said that her fluency had made her a member of the tribe for the duration of her stay.

'Isn't that very odd?'

'Not at all. It's a feature of all known peoples. Language acts as an entry card.'

I listened to Miriam chatting with a housewife. 'Perhaps it's my imagination, but I hear you speaking like a pair of songbirds. It's very pleasing.'

She smiled. 'So you've noticed. The *p* sound doubled.' She outlined the importance of the letter p, the most used and often doubled as *pp*. 'We've been talking about the coloured clay on the floor of her house. *Pparppa* is the word for this. Since the language is agglutinative, she makes it into a double word:

pparppanchatta – to limp like a man who is lame or a bird that can no longer fly. Economic and very poetic, like much of the language.'

Miriam told me what she had learned about children. A mother is usually so hard-working that she arranges for her elder daughter, starting from age five, to teach her siblings from age three to four, while her husband limits teaching to his elder son, who will work beside him with the animals. For the tribe, the language was not written, only spoken, so its complexities could be ignored. Instead of recreation, these children learnt the rules of society by example, helped by a rich oral tradition of funny stories and animal fables, a mixture of moralizing and superstition.

We were joined by Gonzalo and Bernard who had visited the dispensary. 'We talked to the visiting pharmacist from Arica. He brings patent medicines in bottles, which are usually ignored, as well as aspirin. The men ask for medicines of their own compounding, mostly made from local plants. I couldn't identify them but some have a strong smell.'

Bernard interrupted. 'I recognized one of them. Quinine, what missionaries call Jesuits' bark. Very effective.'

Gonzalo related how the pharmacist had described Aymara society. 'Each family possesses a piece of land, however small, and that defines their political standing. Each group of families – usually neighbours and perhaps 500 in all – has a right to speak out in the community assemblies held annually, usually after harvest. Each group has a vote and decisions are taken by majority. They have no leader in any sense of the term. And no word for democracy either: the nearest would be "brotherhood".'

Bernard said he had been able to take stock of Aymara man in the dispensary. 'There were several getting herbal remedies. They wouldn't let me take their chest measurements but I didn't need to. All of them had the femur shorter than the tibia. Longer trunk than us, shorter arms and legs. The rib cage is larger to make way for greater lung capacity. They've adapted to height and cold. You were right, Gonzalo.'

The pharmacist had mentioned a young Chilean from the coastal town of Iquique who was living in the village studying Aymara. Bernard led the way to the edge of the village and we soon found the house, dilapidated with holes in the roof. Its occupant wore a sweatshirt, jeans and running shoes. He spoke English, having learned it at college where he'd shown an aptitude for languages. The archbishop of Iquique had sponsored his year with the Aymara. 'How far have you got with your missionary work?' asked Bernard.

The young man laughed. 'That's the one thing the archbishop has forbidden.'

'Then why are you learning Aymara?'

'To speak it correctly. Only then will the tribe treat me as an equal.'

'But you're being trained as a priest.'

He shook his head and said humbly, 'My name is Pablo but I don't have a vocation. As a layman I may be able to make one or two converts.'

Miriam sighed. 'Poor Bertonio – ten years – how he must have suffered!' She looked our new acquaintance in the eye. 'What is the Aymara attitude to Christianity?'

'They fear Christianity,' Pablo responded at once. 'That's because their belief system is weak. Though their language is exact and robust, their religion can best be described as magic. Take *pachamama*, meaning "mother earth": it's been stretched to mean an omnipotent female god. She produces food and cakes but also receives sacrifices, preferably a llama's foetus. They also sacrifice to other gods. Amaru, the snake, linked to the fertility found in rivers and irrigation channels, and a protective hill: these are both gods. But there is no creator God and they don't feel the need for one. Instead of serious worship, they fool around with magic and potions. In theory they might seem ripe for missionary work. And so it was believed since Bertonio's time. But where he failed, no one else succeeded.

'And so we've had to rethink the Aymara. See them as they really are: a peace-loving people. They don't kill, not even animals for food. They are not promiscuous: they never choose wives outside the forbidden degrees and their marriages always last. They educate their children as best they can. As one of Bertonio's fellow missionaries put it in a book about a tribe similar to the Aymara: "they live and behave like Adam's children in the Garden of Eden. Why do we trouble to convert them?" Yet he continued with his missionary work.'

He paused before resuming. 'Perhaps we should leave the Aymara as they are. Believing that when they die they will go like Adam to a new Paradise. Our learned archbishop considered it but decided on a quite different approach. Can you guess what?'

We were silent. Miriam said bluntly that there could not be a different approach.

'We would praise the Aymara. For their joyful and imaginative fiestas, for their effective herbal remedies, for their villages formed into one brotherhood, for discovering the potato. We would tell them that complex language is the language created by God and imparted to Adam's soul, and by him to his children and their descendants.'

'Exactly right, Pablo. That way, you can speak of a Creator God whom we treat as male, but could reasonably be conceived as female.'

Pablo explained a more sophisticated approach. According to philologists, languages divide into those with a two-value logic (where a sentence is either true or false) or a three-value logic.

The three-value logic draws on abstract concepts and modal subtleties to give a third answer. So, according to two-value logic, the answers to 'Has it stopped raining?' can only be either 'Yes, it has' or 'No, it hasn't.' An answer according to three-value would be, 'It is raining, but it appears to have stopped' where both statements are true. Aymara is a language with three-value logic.

'Our archbishop has put Aymara grammar to good use in the way he teaches doctrine. Take the Trinity – Three Persons in One God. For us that's a mystery which we believe to be true without understanding it. But in the Aymara language it is not a mystery. It is logical that God should be One and also Three. Again with the Resurrection. Christ died and also did not die, because he was God.'

A long pause followed while we took this in. 'I mustn't keep you. Are you staying long?'

'We're going back to Arica almost immediately,' I said.

'But I'm here for a fortnight,' said Miriam. 'I befriended a granny who admired my hat. She said she could put me up.'

Pablo pulled a face. 'Could you really survive on potatoes and *maté* for two whole weeks? Why not lodge here and eat real food? I've a motorbike on which I go to fetch bread and tinned food. You'll still get plenty of opportunities to speak the language.'

So it was agreed. We took our leave of Pablo, and Miriam came back to the car to fetch her bags and say goodbye. Gonzalo hurried us on and whizzed off fast across the grass towards Arica.

CHAPTER EIGHTEEN

Decisions

Next morning, we woke early to Arica's familiar combination of smells. The pong of fish meal and the scent of red oleander mingled together seemed to reflect our conflicting moods. Our variegated journey had left us with much to think about and now we also had to reflect on what lay ahead.

Gonzalo appeared in bad humour; he was vexed that he had initially opposed our visit to the Aymara when he should have been more informed about the cultural importance of this unique tribe. Over breakfast he confided his concerns. Not about whether to testify against his torturer, but what to do about Miriam's parting words to him. 'Put the Aymara in the care of the United Nations,' she had commended. 'Only they have the authority and finances.'

Bernard and I agreed with the sentiment, but we also had misgivings. Protect the Aymara from what? They had no known enemies. And how would the United Nations spare the time and money when they had a score of African tribes on their agenda, all at war because they spoke different languages?

Bernard came up with an answer. 'The United Nations could assemble a group of philologists to prepare an international language. On the lines of Esperanto a hundred years ago. It failed to catch on because it was too provincially European.'

Gonzalo looked to me for a suggestion. 'Preserve the status quo,' I said feebly.

'That's something I cannot do,' he said bleakly. 'I can think of a number of rich and influential men in Santiago who will criticize me if I don't commercialize the Aymara. There's money to be made. Whether it's a ski-ing resort, a state hotel or a gold mine. If I refused to back any of these schemes, I'd come under pressure to resign my job. Frankly, with already one battle to fight I doubt whether I could fight a second.'

We were plunged into deep gloom. Bernard and I exchanged helpless comments. 'We protect the snow tiger and overlook the fate of people.'

'The Aymara are a chosen tribe, like the Jews.'

'The language has no word for cruelty. They wouldn't understand what Santiago would be proposing to do.'

True to form, Gonzalo pressed us on, leaving the issue dangling. We had to catch our flight.

I chose a window seat facing the Pacific. I could still see the coast, but nothing of Arica town, only the wharves, then unspoiled coastline. I looked down at the town of Iquique and thought of its enterprising archbishop. He could be roped into saving the Aymara. The flight down the coastline in the cloudless blue sky conjured up memories of our recent encounters. 'Heaven is Nearer,' I smiled at the description of the observatory as we flew past La Serena, pleased that I'd said my piece, that astronomers should be thinking less about invisible stars and more about our own unique planetary system.

On arrival, Gonzalo suggested we go to his home, away from the city centre, where we could relax and take stock. The house was fairly new. In the hall glass cases displayed specimens of rock and minerals. Gonzalo's wife was out at work and he told the maid to prepare lunch for us. Leafing through his post, he glanced at the newspapers that had piled up in his absence.

'Pinochet has been discovered salting away millions of dollars into bank accounts held abroad,' he announced excitedly. 'The Government is bound to take legal action against him.'

'Is this good news or bad news for Chile?' I asked.

'Extremely good news both for Chile and for me. Since they tried to kidnap me in Arica, I've been worried sick about whether to go ahead with prosecuting my torturers and thereby risk my wife and daughter's safety. If I don't take action, Pinochet's men get away with their crimes and that's been my Catch-22 for the past few days. I couldn't resolve it and now the Government has done it for me. Pinochet will be indicted, he'll lose all his supporters, and then I can go ahead and see my torturers punished.'

He paused and received our congratulations modestly. 'So now you know what I'll be doing in the immediate future. I'll be getting to grips with the Aymara.'

He caught my eye. 'And you'll be plotting whole new neighbourhoods.'

'We would all be happier if we lived more like the Aymara.'

Bernard was standing looking out of the window. Now he spoke with decision. 'I've learned many small things and one big thing of great importance to me. The discovery of a perfect language which may have been spoken by God when breathing soul into Adam. When I return to Paris, I'll check with the State's omnipotent Research Department that they still intend me to kill human embryos, remove their stem cells and implant them in octogenarians with Alzheimer's. Much as I love Paris, I couldn't do that. I'm better off starting afresh. Not in one of America's famous research centres but in Santiago's medical school.'

'Then I expect you'll want to meet the Director of the University Hospital,' suggested Gonzalo unflappably.

'And you, Archie, will be attending tomorrow's Government advisory committee meeting to assess possible sites.'

'It's going to be quite an undertaking,' I said. Drawing Bernard aside, I suggested a plan. 'Gonzalo's given us all his time and knowledge and expertise. How about you invite him to visit in Paris, then he can cross to England and be my guest in Sussex. We'll split the air fares of course. How does that strike you?'

'Will he have the time?'

'Let's try him.'

Bernard put the idea to Gonzalo who looked touched.

'I remember well the café next to your hospital, and my contests of croquet with Archie.'

'Which you won!'

He shrugged. 'I'll have to polish up my game.'

Appendix

A selection of poems by Gabriela Mistral 1889-1957

BALADA

El pasó con otra;
yo le vi pasar.
Siempre dulce el viento
y el camino en paz.
¡Y estos ojos miseros
le vieron pasar!

El va amando a otra
por la tierra en flor.
Ha abierto el espino;
pasa una canción.
¡Y él va amando a otra

por la tierra en flor!

El besó a la otra
a orillas del mar;
resbaló en las olas

BALLAD

He passed by with another woman;
I saw him pass by.
The wind was forever sweet
And the road, peaceful.
And these wretched eyes
beheld him passing by!

He continues loving another woman
Into flowery lands.
The hawthorn has bloomed;
A song slips away.
And he continues loving another
woman
Into flowery lands.

He kissed the other woman
On seashores;
The orange blossom moon

la luna de azahar.
¡Y no untó mi sangre
la extensión del mar!

El irá con otra
por la eternidad.
Habrá cielos dulces.
(Dios quiere callar.)
¡Y él irá con otra
por la eternidad!

LA NUEZ VANA

I

La nuez abolladita
con la que juegas
caída del nogal
no vió la Terra.

La recogí del pasto,
no supo quién yo era.
Tirada al cielo,
no la vió la ciega.

Con ella cogida
y bailé en la era
y no oyó, la sorda,
correr a las yeguas.

Tú no la voltees.
Su noche la duerma.
La partiras llegando
la primavera.

Trembled upon the waves.
And my blood did not anoint
The expansive sea!

He will walk with another woman
Into eternity.
Sweet skies will prevail.
(God desires silence.)
He will journey with another woman
Through eternity!

THE HOLLOW WALNUT

The rippled nut
With which you play,
Fallen from the walnut tree,
Did not bear witness to the Earth.

I found it in the pasture;
It didn't know who I was.
Cast from the sky,
The visionless one was ignorant of its
plight.
With it in my possession,
I danced upon the green,
But it was deaf and did not hear
The horses running.

Don't disturb it.
A season of night lulls it to sleep.
When spring arrives,
You will split it open;

El mundo de Dios
de golpe le entregas
y le gritas su nombre
y el de la Tierra.

You will return it, unaware,
To God's world;
You will shout its name
And the name of the Earth.

II

Pero él la partió
sin más espera,
y vió caer el polvo
de la nuez huera;
se llenó la mano
de muerte negra,
y la lloró y lloró
la noche entera…

But he split it open
Without waiting,
And saw the dust fall
From the hollow walnut:
His hand filled
With dark death,
And he sobbed and sobbed
The entire night.

III

Vamos a sepultarla
bajo unas hierbas,
antes de que se venga
la primavera.
No sea que Dios vivo
en pasando la vea
y toque con sus manos
la muerte en la Tierra.

Let's bury it
Under the grass
Before spring comes.

Perhaps, in passing, the God of life
Will see it,
And with His hands touch
The Earth's dead one.

CARRO DEL CIELO

HEAVEN'S CARRIAGE

Echa atrás la cara, hijo,
y recibe las estrellas
A la primera mirada,
todas te punzan y hielan,
y después el cielo mece

Throw your head back, child,
and receive the stars.
At first sight,
They all sting and chill you,
And then the sky rocks

como cuna que balancan,	Like a cradle that they balance,
y tú te das perdidamente	And at a loss, you give up,
como cosa que llevan y llevan …	Like something carried away and away.
Dios baja para tomarnos	God touches down to take us
en su viva polvareda;	Into the nebula of his life;
cae en el cielo estrellado	He falls into the star-filled sky
como una cascada suelta.	Like a waterfall set free,
Baja, baja en el carro del Cielo,	Descend, descend into Heaven's Carriage,
va a llegar y nunca llega …	It is going to arrive and it never does …
El viene incesentamente	It comes down incessantly
y a media marcha se refrena,	And stops halfway
por amor y miedo de amor	For love and the fear of love
de que nos rompe o que nos ciega.	That breaks or blinds us.
Mientras viene somos felices	While it is en route, we rejoice
y lloramos cuando se aleja.	And we cry when it leaves.
Y un día el carro no para,	And one day the carriage doesn't stop.
ya desciende, ya se acerca,	It continues to descend and draws you near,
y sientes que toca tu pecho	And you feel the live wheel –
la rueda viva, la rueda fresca.	The fresh wheel touches your heart.
Entonces, sube sin miedo	Then rise without fear,
de un solo salto a la rueda,	With a single leap to the wheel,
¡cantando y llorando del gozo	Singing and crying exultantly
con que te toma y que te lleva!	With the One who takes you and carries you away!

Also by Vincent Cronin

The Golden Honeycomb: A Sicilian Quest (1954)
The Wise Man from the West: Matteo Ricci and his Mission to China (1955)
The Last Migration (1957)
A Pearl to India: The Life of Roberto de Nobili (1959)
The Letter After Z (1960)
A Calendar of Saints (1963)
The Companion Guide to Paris (1963)
Louis XIV (1964)
Four Women in Pursuit of an Ideal (1965) (also published as *The Romantic Way*, 1966)
The Florentine Renaissance (1967)
Mary Portrayed (1968)
The Flowering of the Renaissance (1969)
Napoleon (1971) (also published as *Napoleon Bonaparte: An Intimate Biography*, 1972)
The Horizon Concise History of Italy (1972) (also published as *A Concise History of Italy*, 1973)
Louis and Antoinette (1974)
Catherine, Empress of All the Russias (1978)
The View from Planet Earth: Man Looks at the Cosmos (1981)
Paris on the Eve, 1900-1914 (1989)
The Renaissance (1992)
Paris: City of Light, 1919-1939 (1994)